Fulton Co. Public Library
320 W. 7th St.
Rochester, IN 46975

THE MAN
NEXT DOOR

THE MAN NEXT DOOR

•

Bernadette Pruitt

AVALON BOOKS
THOMAS BOUREGY AND COMPANY, INC.
401 LAFAYETTE STREET
NEW YORK, NEW YORK 10003

Library of Congress Catalog Card Number: 98-96612
ISBN 0-8034-9323-1

PRINTED IN THE UNITED STATES OF AMERICA
ON ACID-FREE PAPER
BY HADDON CRAFTSMEN, BLOOMSBURG, PENNSYLVANIA

THE MAN NEXT DOOR

Chapter One

"He's heerrrre!"

Erin March jumped up from her desk in her home office and followed the sound of her niece's voice. She found the four-year-old on tiptoe, peering out a living-room window. Her nose and fingertips were pressed to the screen. Wiggles, their Yorkshire terrier, panted excitedly as he jumped up trying to get a look.

"Who, Lily?" Erin asked.

"The new neighbor man," she said, poking the window with a dimpled finger.

Erin crouched down and squinted through the August sunlight at the saltbox house next door. The shutters were open for the first time in weeks and the front door was flung back. A shiny, dark gray BMW sat in the driveway.

"Maybe it's just the landlord, Pumpkin. I don't think the new tenant is due until next week."

The words were barely out of her mouth when the rumble of an engine filled the air and a dusty orange moving van rolled into view at the end of the street. With a groan and a squeak, it came to a halt in front of the one-and-one-half-story house. Wiggles, his paws a few inches short of the windowsill, threw all of his five pounds into his most ferocious guard dog impersonation.

Erin scooped him up with her arm and patted his silky

coat. ''It's all right, boy,'' she said. ''There's nothing to get excited about.''

''You mean it's not him?'' Lily asked. The low afternoon sunlight cast a coppery rim of light around her sable brown Dutch-boy-style haircut. Large green eyes, fringed with thick lashes, peered curiously from under her bangs.

Erin studied the truck a moment longer. ''Maybe it is, after all.''

She watched the driver, a Goliath of a man, spring from the cab. He was joined by a partner who appeared even shorter than Erin's five feet, four inches. Despite the mismatched team that they were, they had the rear of the truck opened in seconds and were carting with apparent ease a bulky object in brown wrapping paper up the brick path leading into the house. For an instant, a shadowy form appeared in the doorway.

''There he is,'' Lily said, bouncing on her toes. ''I'll ask him if he's the new neighbor man.'' She broke away from the window in a blur.

Erin's heart kicked as she caught her by hooking a finger between the straps of her faded denim overalls

''Wait, Lily,'' she called as the dog lurched out of her arm. Erin pulled her close. ''Now is not the time. You and Wiggles can watch from the window, but don't go outside. It's dangerous with all those heavy things being moved. In a day or two, after he's settled in a bit, we can welcome him to the neighborhood.''

The child gave a reluctant nod, then looked glumly out the window. The movers were carrying another bundle, this one shaped like a desk.

''Do you think he has any toys?'' Lily asked, leaning against the windowsill.

Erin knelt beside her again. ''Probably not, honey.''

Lily turned toward her. ''Mr. and Mrs. Swayze had toys when they lived there.''

''But they were special friends,'' Erin said consolingly. ''They kept them just for you and Wiggles.''

Lily's lower lip jutted out. ''I don't want a new neighbor. I want the Swayzes back.''

''I know,'' Erin said, pulling the child into her embrace, ''but the Vermont winters were getting too hard on Mrs. Swayze. She was having a terrible time with her arthritis. Think of how much better the warm Florida sunshine will be for her, and you won't feel so sad. Besides, they promised to come back and visit every summer. And, perhaps later, if business is better, we can go visit them.''

Lily sniffed and wiped a tear away with the back of her hand. Erin took a tissue from the pocket of her black-and-white-checked jumper and touched it to the child's face. Her heart wrenched. For such a little girl, she'd already been through so much. If only she could shield her from any more losses.

''Why don't we set up your little table in front of the window?'' she asked. ''You can watch the movers while you draw a picture to mail to the Swayzes. I'll get you a snack while you get your crayons.''

''Okay,'' she said, with a trace of tears still in her voice. She marched toward her bedroom with Wiggles at the heels of her red high-top sneakers.

Erin closed her eyes and took a deep breath. Lily's hurts were hers as well. Even though she was her brother's child, she couldn't imagine loving her more if she were her own. Now, since Stephen's death, Lily was hers, she reminded herself. The thought of being solely responsible for her kept her awake for hours some nights. But despite the worries that the spunky little girl could bring, she was the light of Erin's life.

Erin carried the child-sized wooden table from Lily's bedroom and placed it in front of the window. The table was blue and painted with Bavarian folk art. When she was a buyer for an import company, she'd found it in a village near the German-Austrian border. She brought in one of the matching chairs and glanced out the window. A man silhouetted against the slanting rays of the sun stood on the sidewalk. She studied him through the parted lace curtains, but she was unable to discern much except that he was tall and wore sunglasses. She watched as the smaller member of the moving team handed him what appeared to be bills of lading. Suddenly, the taller man turned toward her window and she jerked back as a warming flush spread over her cheeks. She could only hope that he only sensed someone was watching, that he couldn't actually see that she was really there. She felt silly, but after all, newcomers didn't often come to Maple Springs, Vermont. Yet, for that matter, hardly anyone left, with many residents having roots that reached back several centuries.

Lily entered, wagging a small box of crayons. A sketch pad was tucked under her other arm. "I'm going to draw a picture and put it in a you-see'em."

Erin smiled, remembering the museum they'd gone to not long ago. She helped her arrange the art supplies on the table and pulled out a small chair for her. "I'll be right back with your snack."

Lily, who resumed peering out the window, seemed not to hear her. Erin dashed to the kitchen, put three vanilla wafers on a plate, and poured a small mug of milk. She set them on the little table. "Make some nice pictures while I work. I've gotten behind today and I have some important orders to look after. I'm going to be very busy for a while, but this evening, we can do something together.''

She gave the little girl a quick kiss on the crown. Lily was long accustomed to this routine. Erin tended to her home-based business, Dream House Imports, Inc., while Lily busied herself with play projects.

Erin returned to the spare bedroom she'd converted into an office and sat behind the long, scrub pine table that served as her desk. A computer sat on one end and a stack of invoices on the other. A faded red-and-blue Oriental rug that she'd once lugged back from Turkey lay across the oak floor. The rug had been for a client who not only decided she wanted a Chinese rug instead but had changed her whole color scheme during Erin's buying trip. Above the window was a swag of Irish lace, another souvenir of her short but stimulating career with Karim Imports. Brass-framed sketches of European street scenes lined the walls. Antique delft tiles from Holland were displayed on the childproof top shelf of a floor-to-ceiling bookcase.

They were all reminders of her life before Lily. Fresh out of college with a degree in interior design, Erin managed to land a job with a Boston import company. She started with an office job, keeping track of shipments of tartans from Scotland and batiks from Indonesia. Finally, after a long apprenticeship, she was given her own account, and that involved making buying trips to Europe and the Middle East.

It was in Ireland that she met Jonathan Garrick, an American businessman doing consulting for an Irish firm. Erin was immediately taken by his blond and boyish good looks and zest for life. Hardly the staid company vice president, he'd once rented a motorcycle with which to show her Dublin's quaint nooks and crannies. Back in Boston, he was apt to surprise her by bringing over pizza at midnight. To Erin, who had lost both her parents by the time she was twenty, he was the joy that had been missing from her life. He was a man of the moment, impulsive yet charming, a man with a boy's exuberance for life. As it turned out, he was to prove more boy than man. But by then, it was too late. Erin had already lost her heart to him.

They were making wedding plans when Erin was called back to Vermont to face a family tragedy. Her brother, Stephen, a struggling potter of growing reputation, and his wife, Carrie, a potter as well, had both died in a two-car crash on a twisting mountain road during a pummeling rainstorm. They left behind Lily, then two, who had been left with a sitter so they could attend a pottery show. Along with the carload of pottery, the accident had crushed the dreams of two young and loving parents who wanted to see their daughter grow up simply and happily.

Erin was devastated. She and Stephen had been so close that she had driven to Maple Springs from Boston twice a month to visit her baby niece. She spent vacations in the old bungalow that they had partially converted into a studio, with a kiln in a backyard shed. Her love for Lily sometimes amazed her. She found herself thinking with pride of all her little milestones—her first steps, her first words.

From the beginning, the bond between aunt and niece was special. The child, named for Stephen and Erin's mother, was given Erin's name for a middle name. So when Stephen and Carrie died, Erin didn't hesitate to seek guardianship of the baby. Since she'd been Lily's second mother of sorts, she anticipated no problems. But there were two, and they were daunting. They tested all the reserve she had left. First, Jonathan delivered the stunning blow of breaking their engagement. He was only prepared to marry one person, he'd said, not two. Next, Stephen's wife's sister and brother-in-law also filed for guardianship of Lily. Although they'd shown little interest in the child in the past, they'd contended they were better suited for the job. They were wealthy, had an established home, and there were two of them versus one of Erin.

The next few months were a nightmare. Erin took a leave of absence from her job and moved into Stephen and Carrie's house, which she now occupied. Although mortgaged, it was the only financial asset they had. Stephen had had no life insurance. She hired a lawyer to argue her case. After all, she was the one Lily knew and loved. Putting her in the hands of two strangers would be traumatic.

The Holbrookes, Mallory and Yale, were a childless two-career couple in their late thirties with all the requisite Yuppie status symbols—designer clothing, a house in a fashionable neighborhood, and a vehicle for each bay of their three-car garage. They'd promised the best of nannies for little Lily. Their attorney had the same sort of Boston polish and aloofness. His wire-rimmed glasses, perfectly styled hair, and impeccably tailored suits spelled out his difficulty relating to the free-spirit background from which Lily had come. Remembering his arguments still brought the sting of indignation to Erin's cheeks. ''Your Honor, Erin March is single and of very limited means. She owns no home. In fact, she's a globe-trotter—hardly at home at all. She's hardly more than a girl herself, and Europe and the Middle East, not the nursery, are her playground. This is not what Lily March needs. This child deserves a stable home environment with two parents and Yale and Mallory Holbrooke can best provide it for her.''

Erin came so close to jumping up and making a rebuttal herself that her lawyer had to yank her back to her seat.

How dare he make her sound like some careless playgirl? His tone oozed with skepticism and disdain. She was an efficient and responsible businesswoman who traveled for work, not pleasure, although the latter couldn't be avoided. She was willing to sacrifice her career for Lily. How dare he?

Although the grandmotherly judge had ultimately seen things Erin's way, it was hard to forget the Holbrookes' attorney's stinging rhetoric.

When the decision was rendered, Erin wept with joy and relief. She expected the couple to file an appeal, but nothing of that sort had yet happened. In fact, in the two years since Erin had had Lily, they had only come to visit her once. Yet Erin still had nightmares about the Holbrookes and their icy Boston lawyer taking the little girl away.

In order to stay home with Lily as much as possible, Erin started her own business, supplying interior decorators and shop owners with home accessories from around the world. But despite her contacts, the business wasn't easy to get off the ground. At the end of her second year as president of Dream House Imports, Inc., Erin was barely making enough for her and Lily to live on. Today, she was counting on a large shipment of Polish pottery to provide enough extra cash to fix the roof before winter.

As she prepared a fax to a Burlington decorator who was losing patience waiting for the pottery to arrive, Erin peered around the doorway to check on Lily who was scribbling at the little table with a fat red crayon. She turned back to the fax machine but was interrupted by the telephone.

"Dream House Imports," she answered.

The faint, crackling noises on the line told her it was an international phone call. "Ereeen," a heavily accented female voice said, "Katarzyna Pasakowski from Krakow."

"Katie!" Erin greeted. "I was just thinking about you because my pottery shipment is due this week."

There was a brief pause on the other end of the line. "Ereeen, that's why I called you on the telephone. I am afraid the shipment might have been stolen."

A knot formed in Erin's stomach. "Stolen?" she asked numbly.

"We just learned that there were some thefts at the port and your shipment was among the things missing."

Erin dropped into her chair. "Oh, no," she said. "I was counting on this."

"I'm so sorry, Ereeen." Her voice was filled with sympathy. "I will get another shipment to you as soon as I can, but it might be two months."

Erin's spine stiffened. "Why so long?"

"The family that has the workshop goes on holiday in August—for the entire month. They shut everything down."

Her shoulders sagged as she sank further into her chair.

She imagined the family of Polish potters frolicking on a sunny beach while bill collectors rapped on her own door. "What a bummer," she exclaimed.

"Pardon me. I don't think I know that word," Katarzyna responded.

"I'm sorry," Erin said. "It's an American expression that means something like bad luck."

"Oh, yes, I understand. Oh, I am very sorry once more. The moment the Rybickis return. I will tell them to please, hurry, get your order."

"Thank you, Katie."

"Good-bye."

Erin put the receiver down with a thump of frustration. How was she going to explain this to her fussy new client—one she had spent months trying to win over with promises of first-rate service? Raymond Didier, of Didier Interiors, was going to scream at the top of his French-Canadian lungs.

She buried her face in her hands and shook her head, her straight, chin-length blond hair swinging from side to side. She sucked in a deep breath as she reached for her client list. Before picking up the phone, she stepped to the doorway to check on Lily once again. This time, she found the child's chair empty. A charmingly crude rendering of the saltbox next door lay on the table.

Her stomach tightened. "Lily?"

When there was no response, Erin checked the other rooms, then the backyard. The child's swing, hung from a thick bough of an old oak, was likewise empty. Erin's heart thumped in alarm. "Lily!" she called, but only silence ensued.

She raced back into the house and looked out the living-room window at the saltbox. The front door was closed, the moving van gone. She'd turned toward the door to make a sweep of the front yard, when the front door opened. Wiggles scurried in, followed by Lily. The child's face was red and tear-streaked.

Erin rushed to her and fell to one knee. "Lily, what's wrong? Where have you been?"

The little girl sniffed as she wiped a tear away with the back of her hand. "The new neighbor man's. He doesn't like us. He made us come home."

The spring of tension inside Erin tightened. "Pumpkin, you weren't supposed to go over there, remember?"

"I know, Aunt Erin, but when I opened the front door to watch the moving truck leave, Wiggles ran over there. The door was open and he went inside. I had to get him."

''Oh, dear,'' Erin said, taking the child into her arms. The Swayzes had been like grandparents to Lily and had maintained almost an open-door policy. They kept treats for the dog and encouraged daily visits.

''Wiggles just wanted to visit,'' Lily said. ''He didn't mean to do that other thing.''

Erin's stomach tightened as she held the little girl at arm's length. ''What other thing?'' she asked, glancing down at Wiggles. The little terrier's black eyes sparkled innocently back at her. ''What do you mean?'' she asked with a gulp. She imagined a priceless Oriental carpet damaged, and feared the worst.

''He ate part of the neighbor man's sandwich,'' she said tearfully.

Erin breathed a partial sigh of relief. A sandwich was certainly easier to replace than a rug.

''He didn't mean it, honest,'' she continued.

''Of course not, honey,'' she said with a comforting squeeze. ''What did the man say to you?''

''He said to go home. He was an ol' slouch.''

''You mean grouch?''

Lily, her eyes round and luminous, nodded with a sniff. ''A big ol' slouchy grouch.''

''Did you tell him you were sorry?''

''I tried, but he wouldn't listen. He put us out on the porch and shut the door.''

Erin bristled. She couldn't blame him for being annoyed over the sandwich, but he did seem to have some of the markings of a ''big ol' slouchy grouch.'' Nevertheless, a formal apology was in order.

''Let's go over and tell him you and Wiggles are sorry,'' she said.

But just as she pulled open the front door, the telephone rang. ''Oh, dear, let me get that first.''

Erin ran into her office, her heart racing, and glanced at her watch. The afternoon was almost gone and she'd accomplished little. She snatched up the receiver. ''Dream House Imports. Erin March speaking.''

''Miss March,'' said an affected male voice that she immediately recognized as belonging to Raymond Didier. ''I don't know if you keep count, but this is the third time I've called to inquire about my pottery shipment.'' There was an edge of impatience in his voice.

Erin's stomach wrapped itself into a four-square knot. ''Yes, you have every right to inquire, as any good businessman would,'' she said, trying to soften the blow she was about to deliver. ''I'm very sorry, but I just learned this afternoon that the shipment may not arrive before October.''

''What?'' he screeched.

Erin winced. ''The crate containing the original shipment was stolen from the port. The order will have to be remade,'' she said, explaining the situation in detail.

''You assured me that you had reliable contacts,'' he said huffily. ''Imagine,'' he snorted, ''an entire workshop shutting down for a month. What kind of operation are we dealing with here?''

Erin's chest was so tight that she could barely breathe. ''It's one of the oldest and best pottery works in Europe,'' she said. ''I'm terribly sorry, Mr. Didier. I'm as upset as you are. The theft was beyond our control.''

''That will be of little comfort to my clients,'' he said. ''Now what am I going to do? The cottage look is all the rage and that particular pottery was perfect for it. It was to be the finishing touch for several of my current projects.

Now I'll have to wait months to get the final installment of my fees. This does not please me, Miss March. I have bills to pay, like everyone else."

Her cheeks tingled. "I will do everything I can to expedite delivery."

"Do that," he retorted, "because it might just be the last order you get from me. I have lots of contacts in this business, you know."

Erin's chest tightened even more, almost cutting off her wind. "You have my word I'll do everything humanly possible."

"Good," he said, before hanging up with a snap.

Erin limply placed the receiver back on the phone. Her fingers went immediately to her throbbing temples. The new account with the largest decorating firm in Vermont was evaporating like mist in the sun.

Suddenly, her thoughts jumped back to Lily. She dashed into the living room but there was no sign of her or the dog.

"Lily!" she called, making a quick sweep of the house. She had just turned toward the backyard when the front doorbell rang.

She did a quick about-face and rushed to the front door. She flung it open to find a man standing on the front porch. In one arm was Lily, who was again in tears. Tucked in the crook of the other was Wiggles.

"Are these yours? he asked. His rich baritone contained a hint of impatience and an echo of something vaguely familiar.

Erin felt a mixture of alarm and relief. "Yes," she said, opening the screen door.

He set child and dog down. "You might want to keep a

better eye on them. My house,'' he said, glancing toward the saltbox, ''is not the lost and found.''

Erin pulled Lily to her. ''I'm terribly sorry,'' she said, studying him warily.

He was six feet, if not a little taller, and outfitted in jeans and a denim shirt, sleeves rolled up at the elbows. He appeared to be in his mid-thirties. Strands of thick dark hair, touched with silver, fluttered over his forehead in the summer breeze. His face was framed by a closely cropped beard. His stormy, deep blue gaze swept over her once, and then again, the second time with a strong hint of puzzlement.

Uncomfortable under his scrutiny, Erin took a half step back inside the doorway.

''I would appreciate it if you would rein in the welcome wagon,'' he continued. ''They've already done enough for one day. The dog ate my sandwich—the only thing I've had to eat all day—and the child dropped two days' worth of work into a bucket of soapy water.''

Erin stared at him in confusion. ''Work? I don't understand,'' she said as Lily clung to the skirt of her jumper. Wiggles circled the man's worn-out running shoes and yapped.

''She dropped a computer disk into a bucket I was using to wipe up footprints the movers left behind. The disk contained pages of important notes I'd taken. It was the last straw,'' he said, his eyes narrow with disapproval.

''I'm sorry. I didn't mean it,'' Lily said, giving Erin a pleading look with her huge green eyes. They brimmed with tears all over again. ''I was just looking at it and it slipped.''

The man's piercing gaze softened slightly. Despite the annoyance they contained, Erin couldn't help but notice that his eyes were strikingly handsome. "It—it's all right," he said. Seemingly uncomfortable, he quickly diverted his eyes back to Erin. "I think I know you," he said. "Aren't you Erin March?"

Her lips parted in surprise. "Yes," she finally managed to say.

He held out a large, square hand.

"I represented the other side in the guardianship case. I'm Wyatt Keegan."

Chapter Two

Erin's heart stalled in her chest. Everything else seemed to stop as well. The air turned still, Lily quit crying, and the dog ceased barking, as she, as motionless as the columns holding up the front porch, studied the man in stunned realization.

Of course. His beard followed the lines of the square and stern jaw that she recalled, but obscured a cleft in his chin. Before, his eyes had been hidden behind glasses that had given him a handsomely bookish air. His hair, then groomed to perfection, was now tousled and shot through with silver. But his broad shoulders and commanding voice still spelled out the same powerful presence, one that put Erin on her guard.

She steeled herself with a deep breath. "You're acting more like W. C. Fields. I hope you didn't tell Lily and Wiggles to go play in the street."

His lower lip jutted out in rebuke. "No, but I did tell them to go home, and before I knew it, the little boomerangs came back."

Erin's cheeks blazed. "I'm sorry, I did my best to keep them away, but Lily only went after Wiggles. The people who used to live there had them over every afternoon."

"I want Grandma and Grandpa Swayze back," Lily wailed.

Wyatt blinked. Erin cringed inwardly, touching a quieting finger to her lips.

"I don't remember there being any grandparents," he said stiffly.

"The Swayzes were like grandparents. Lily doesn't have any of her own except for her mother's father and he—well, he leads an active singles life in Florida."

"Oh, yes," Wyatt said, a hint of mirth in his eyes, "the merry widower."

"He's a very nice man," Erin said defensively, smoothing Lily's dark, glossy hair.

"And I suppose you think I'm not," he added wryly.

Erin, cocking her head to one side, offered no argument.

Wyatt took a deep breath. "Erin, I'm not really such a bad guy. But nobody likes the only meal they've had all day snarfed up by a dog, or finding an important computer disk swimming in a pail of soapy water."

Lily's sobbing started anew, and a pained, guilty look spread over his face. "Women, no matter how young, know how to get to a man, don't they?"

He dropped to one knee. "I'm sorry," he said, touching a finger to her tear-streaked cheek. "I know you didn't mean to do it."

"Wiggles didn't either," Lily sniffed.

"No, of course not," he said, rising to his full height. "Do you promise to keep a better eye on Wiggles?"

Lily nodded eagerly.

"Good." He glanced reproachfully at Erin. "Do you promise to keep a better eye on this child?"

Erin, feeling the sting of chastisement on her cheeks, gave a stiff nod. "Please, accept our apology."

He gave a curt nod. "And now, if you'll excuse me, I have some unpacking to do."

Before she could respond, the ring of the telephone cut through the air.

''Wait please,'' she said, before he could reach the first step leading off the porch. ''There's something I would like to ask you. Would you mind coming in for just a moment?''

He hesitated, studying her with deliberation. ''Make it brief. I'd like to get away before anything else happens.''

''Of course,'' she said nervously. ''Come, Lily,'' she said, taking the child by the hand, and hurrying into the house, ''let's not bother Mr. Keegan.''

After offering him a seat on the sofa, she rushed to the telephone.

''Miss March, it's Raymond Didier again. . . .''

Erin's muscles kinked at the sound of his voice. ''Yes, Mr. Didier,'' she said breathlessly. ''How can I be of service?''

''I would like for you to cancel my pottery order.''

His words came at her like a rockslide. ''Cancel the order?'' she finally managed to say. ''Are you sure?''

''Certain,'' he said haughtily. ''I have found another source through another import firm.''

Erin wilted to a seated position on the corner of her desk. ''But I have an exclusive contract with Krakow Pottery in the state of Vermont.''

''You're quite correct, my dear, but that doesn't stop me from getting it out of New York. I know this problem was beyond your control, but I must do what's best for me and my clients.''

''I understand, Mr. Didier, and I'm very sorry,'' she said, her voice flat with disappointment. ''I hope we can still do business in the future.''

''Perhaps.'' His tone was unconvincing.

Erin hung up with a sigh. If she were alone, she might consider venting her frustration with a good bloodcurdling scream, but with Wyatt Keegan in the next room, it didn't seem like a good idea.

She straightened her shoulders, put as pleasant a look on her face as she could muster, despite the fact that an important account had just been torpedoed, and went to face her next problem—him.

He was nibbling gingerly at the corner of a bulging sandwich. Jelly oozed from the opposite corner onto a plate he held under it. Lily sat next to him wearing a satisfied smile and dribbles of peanut butter and jelly on the front of her overalls. On the other side of him was Wiggles, his eyes trained on the snack.

"I made the neighbor man another sandwich," Lily announced brightly.

Wyatt swallowed with difficulty. "It was very thoughtful of her," he said chokingly. "I didn't realize it was possible to get so much peanut butter between two slices of bread."

Erin blinked at the two-inch-thick concoction. "Yes, that was nice of you, Lily. Now, go wipe off the front of your overalls before you get jelly on the furniture. Take your time and do a good job. And when you finish, feed Wiggles."

"Do I have to right now?" she asked. "I'd rather stay here with Mr. Keegan."

Wyatt winced almost imperceptibly.

"Yes, you have to," she said firmly.

The little girl scooted off the sofa and trudged off, head bowed, toward the bathroom.

Wyatt laid the sandwich down. "She's a handful, isn't she?" he asked, once the child was out of sight.

The question brought back raw memories of a gray-suited Wyatt questioning, before a judge, her ability to handle a child by herself. ''Most four-year-olds are,'' she said defensively. ''Do you know much about children?''

His eyes darkened and he glanced away. ''No,'' he said, his voice tight. ''Is that what you intended to ask me?''

Erin pulled a wicker rocker closer to the sofa and sat down. ''You know what I'd like to ask?'' she said, leaning forward. She lowered her voice. ''Why are you in Maple Springs? How is it that we are suddenly next-door neighbors?''

He glanced distractedly about the room with its odd mix of small, mismatched Oriental rugs, a hand-painted armoire from Austria, a mantel display of platters from England, nesting dolls from Russia, and a farm wagon from Germany. He then turned toward her, crossing one long leg over the other. In a room that reflected decidedly feminine tastes, he seemed incongruous with his surroundings. A lace curtain fluttered at the window next to one broad shoulder. The tailored needlepoint cushion beside him suddenly appeared dainty. Erin was unaccustomed to so much masculinity packed into one small room.

''It's simple,'' he said, finally. ''I'm going to practice law here for a little while. Nathan Webber of Webber, Steadman and Hartley is an old friend of mine. He's going to teach in Boston for a semester and I agreed to take over his practice until the middle of December.''

Lily, the bib of her overalls soaked, scampered back into the living room, followed by the dog. But as she plopped down next to Wyatt, Erin detected a sudden hint of strain in his expression.

Erin placed a finger on her lips to signal that she was to be silent and on her best behavior.

''As for the house,'' he continued, ''Nate knew the man

who bought this house from your neighbors. Since the owner won't need it himself until he retires, he wanted to rent it out for a short time. So here I am, the convenient tenant.''

''How nice,'' Erin said with a ring of skepticism. ''Is that the whole story?''

A hint of amusement danced in his eyes. The beard drew attention to their mysterious deep blue depths. ''Is this an interview for the position of next-door neighbor?''

His penetrating gaze left her feeling unsettled. ''It seems you've already gotten the job.''

He responded with a wry smile. ''Yes, and what a challenging job it's going to be.''

''What does challenging mean?'' Lily interjected, swinging her feet against the sofa.

Erin stared at him in an unspoken dare to explain it to the child.

''Your aunt will be happy to explain it to you later,'' he said, his eyes not leaving Erin's face.

Erin bristled.

''You didn't eat all your sandwich,'' the little girl said, giving the crust a poke with a pudgy finger. There was a hint of disappointment in her voice.

Wyatt cleared his throat nervously. ''You wouldn't mind if I took it home and finished it, would you? There might even be enough for supper and breakfast both.''

''Oh, yes, you can take it home,'' she said merrily, thrusting sandwich and plate at him. The plate tipped against his chest, leaving a blob of grape jelly on the front of his shirt. Wyatt winced. Lily clamped her hand over her mouth.

''Oops!'' Erin said, jumping up. ''Let me get something.''

She darted into the bathroom and returned with a wet washcloth. "I'm so sorry." Accustomed to wiping Lily's spills, she automatically began dabbing at the stain. For an instant, she felt his heartbeat through the soft fabric of his shirt. Her fingertips burned at the touch of the firm muscles of his chest.

"I can manage that," he said, taking the cloth from her fingers.

She pulled away, her cheeks tingling. "Of course. I'll wrap the sandwich." She took the plate and bustled into the kitchen.

Once out of his sight, she collapsed against the counter and emitted a deep, shuddering sigh. She had to get him out of the house before anything else happened. Of all people to move next door, she thought, darkly, as she wrapped the sandwich in foil. She placed the plate in the sink, not wanting to give him an excuse to come back.

When she reentered the living room, he was guardedly holding the picture Lily had drawn of his house.

"A gift from Lily," he explained. "I don't suppose I'll be getting a housewarming gift from you." There was a mischievous glint in his eyes.

Erin cast him a wary glance. "I'm sorry for the inconvenience we've caused you today," she said, ignoring his comment. She handed him the sandwich. As he took it, their fingers touched, sending an unwanted tingling through her.

"Apology accepted," he said. "I won't be so careless as to leave my door open again."

Erin stood stiffly in the doorway, her fists balled inside her jumper pockets, as he strode home across her front lawn. A heavy feeling settled over her while the old memories rushed back. He'd fought hard to keep her from getting Lily, presenting her to the court as a mere girl unready for the responsibilities of raising a child. And now, he was next door, no doubt having gotten a bad impression of all of them, Wiggles included. He'd no doubt also gotten some indication of her business problems. She worried her bottom lip as she grappled with the implications of it.

"Do you already know the new neighbor man?" Lily asked.

Her stomach tensed as she turned toward the little girl. She stood with her arms folded under the bib of her overalls. One sneaker was untied.

Erin knelt to tie the child's shoe, seizing the moment to stall. Lily knew the story of how she had come to live with her. But trying to explain Wyatt's role would only confuse and worry her. "I met him in Boston when you were a baby," she explained simply.

"Was he your boyfriend?"

The irony of the question brought a murmur of laughter to her throat as she stood up. "No," she said, shaking her head. "He's just someone I did some business with once."

"What did he buy?" she persisted with a drawl of innocence.

Erin quirked a corner of her mouth as her heart gave a little skip. "Nothing, as it turned out."

"Oh," Lily said, wandering off toward her crayons.

Erin breathed a sigh of relief and stepped back into her office, but before she could pick up the telephone, Lily appeared.

"What did he want to buy?" she persisted.

Erin blinked, then hesitated. She never wanted to lie to Lily. "Pumpkin, that was a long time ago," she said evasively.

She fidgeted with all of a four-year-old's unspent energy. "Aunt Erin, are me and Wiggles in big trouble?"

"No, just medium-sized trouble. From now on, it's best that you and Wiggles not go next door unless you're invited. We don't want to cause any more problems for Mr. Keegan. It makes him grouchy."

"He's not a big, BIG grouch," Lily said, stretching out her arms. "He liked my sandwich. He 'pologized."

A little smile sneaked onto Erin's lips. "Of course, he did," she said, giving her a hug. "We'll talk more about it later. Now, go put away your playthings."

Erin wished she could be as forgiving as Lily, as the little girl scampered out of the room. She knew that Wyatt Keegan had a courtroom role to play, but he had done it so convincingly that there was no doubt as to his feelings in the case.

She was jarred out of her courtroom memories by the slam of a car door. Lily, her dark bangs flying, raced to the front door.

"It's Tab-i-tha!" she sang, pressing her nose to the screen.

Erin's flagging spirits lifted as she stepped out onto the front porch. The old woman, dressed in her customary jeans, plaid shirt, and hiking boots, traipsed up the sidewalk from her battered four-wheel-drive. She carried a green canvas briefcase trimmed with leather. Erin knew it contained copies of financial records from Dream House Imports.

Lily rushed past Erin and threw her arms around the woman's waist.

"Well, hello, Miss Lily." Her clear alto voice was bigger than she was, gaining strength from seventy years of New England winters. Widowed at an early age, she'd raised a son alone while running a general store that had been in her family for four generations. She was barely over five feet, but Erin had seen her hoist fifty-pound sacks of feed as if they weren't much heavier than a baby. She was not only Erin's part-time bookkeeper and tax accountant, but a special friend as well.

She looked up at Erin and smiled. Her lined cheeks were bronzed from the summer sun. Her hair, once a fiery red, was now a wild cap of bright silver. "This little sprout is shooting right up," she said, ruffling Lily's hair.

"I wish you could say the same thing about my accounts," Erin said. "Come in and have some tea."

It was just past the end of the fiscal year and time for a financial review of the business. Tabitha, followed by Lily and Wiggles, put her briefcase on the long pine table in the dining room and unzipped it.

"We got a new neighbor man," Lily announced.

"Is that so?" Tabitha asked with exaggerated curiosity.

Erin responded with a worried nod. "A Boston lawyer."

She let Lily recount the recent events before sending her out to her sandbox. "Tabitha and I are going to go over the accounts," she explained. "I'll call you in before she leaves."

Once Lily was outside, Erin took a deep breath. "Tabitha, the lawyer is Wyatt Keegan, the one who represented the Holbrookes when they tried to get guardianship of Lily."

The old woman's eyes narrowed. "The one who made you sound like an international playgirl?"

Erin nodded ruefully.

"What a coincidence," the old woman responded.

Erin grimaced. "It's so much of a coincidence that it worries me, Tabitha. He says he's just filling in for Nate

Webber while he teaches in Boston for a semester, but why is he next door? It's not the only house for rent in Maple Springs."

Tabitha bit her bottom lip. "Now that you mention it, I remember Nate's secretary mentioning something about him at the store. A single man in his thirties, she said."

"That's him," Erin said.

"Well, honey," she said, patting Erin's hand, "I wouldn't worry about it. In terms of there being other houses for rent, you may be right. But most aren't this nice. His being here is probably just one of life's little twists. Besides, that case was settled long ago. Those folks have gone off on their own way by now."

Erin sighed. "I know, but the sooner he's gone, the better I'll feel," she said, explaining the day's events. "He's no doubt already convinced he lives next door to a madhouse, that he'd been right about me all along."

"Honey, with kids, anything can happen," Tabitha said reassuringly. "Don't blame yourself. You're wonderful with that child. Now, tell me how the rest of your day went."

Erin frowned. "Awful. I lost the Didier account, the one that took me a year to get."

"Oh, dear," Tabitha said, after hearing the details. Her voice was filled with sympathy. "I'm afraid your fourth-quarter report may not cheer you up much."

Erin chewed a thumbnail as Tabitha opened her ledger on the table. "Let's have it," she said.

"The good news is," the old woman said, pointing a knotty finger at the carefully scripted numbers, "that you're in the black. That's good for a business that's only two years old. But the bad news is that revenues are down ten percent from this time last year."

Erin's heart sank. She studied the figures disconcertedly. "But I've worked so hard, even harder than last year."

"Don't be discouraged, honey," she said. "That's business. It goes up, it goes down."

Erin swallowed hard. "But another downhill slide like that and I may be forced to go back to Boston to work. The worst part would be to have to be away from Lily all day."

Tabitha shook her head. "There were years that I barely squeaked by, and look at me. I'm here."

Erin stood up and gave the woman a quick hug. "I don't know what I'd do without you."

"Nonsense," she said. "You'd do just fine without me."

But despite Tabitha's reassurances, Erin felt discomforted by the day's events. As the old Wagoneer rattled off into the distance, Erin glanced about the bungalow. A wavy brown ring on the dining-room ceiling reminded her that the roof needed replacing. So did the furnace and the car. But everything would have to wait.

Later that evening, after she had put Lily to bed, she returned to her office, as she usually did, to take care of the myriad odds and ends of business. But her mind kept going back to Wyatt Keegan.

She chewed uneasily on a pencil. She'd bungled the situation badly. She'd behaved as if he'd had no reason to complain and she'd dismissed the loss of his computer disk with a bare-bones apology. He must have seen her as one of those irresponsible parents who defend their children's misdeeds. It was hardly a proper way to welcome anyone to a neighborhood. There it was if he wanted to make something of it—a seemingly undisciplined child running amok; a seemingly careless guardian. And to make matters worse, he might have deduced from Mr. Didier's ill-timed phone call that her business didn't provide the greatest measure of financial security for Lily. The Holbrookes would certainly be interested in knowing about that.

Erin shifted uneasily in her chair. She didn't trust this polished Boston barrister with the sub-zero personality. Some damage control was in order.

The next afternoon, after carefully making a sauce of plum tomatoes and herbs and grating three kinds of cheese, Erin took her peace offering out of the oven. It was lasagna, made from her own recipe. She could only hope the fuss-budget wasn't allergic to one of the ingredients.

Since Wyatt had all but declared his house a child- and dog-free zone, Erin drove Lily and Wiggles to the Penobscot General Store to be under Tabitha's watchful eye. When she returned, she put a tomato and fresh basil garnish on the casserole and placed the dish in a wicker basket lined with a red-and-white-checked cloth. Then she went to work on herself, putting on a green print jumper, a white T-shirt, and a touch of makeup.

With basket in hand, she paused at the front door to compose herself. She was going to make a decent impression, no matter what, she vowed. Then, determinedly, she marched across her ragged lawn onto his perfectly manicured turf.

His windows were wide open, but the front door was solidly shut. She faced it squarely and rang the bell, setting off a melodious chime that brought a pang of nostalgia for the Swayzes. She listened for a response, but there was none. She punched the bell again. This time, it was followed by a clatter ending with a loud, dull thump.

"Darn, ouch!" she heard through an open window. "Darn!"

Erin heard approaching footsteps, but they were oddly

arrhythmic. Suddenly, the door snapped open and Wyatt appeared. The beard was gone and in its place was a grimace so sharp that she took a step backward.

''Did I come at a bad time?'' she asked cautiously.

He bit a corner of his mouth and stared at her for a moment from the cool depths of his midnight blue eyes. Then he took one hand from behind his back and produced a fat, red crayon.

''Does this belong to anyone you know?''

''It looks like Lily's,'' she said.

''Put it away before it kills someone,'' he said, rubbing the lower part of his back.

Erin blinked. ''What do you mean?''

He dropped it ceremoniously into one of the large patch pockets on the front of her jumper, took her by the wrist, and led her inside. He faced a staircase leading from the hallway. ''I stepped on it as I was rushing down the stairs to answer the door. I have, if the throbbing accounts for anything, a huge bruise on my backside. Would you care to see the evidence?''

Erin shot him a look of indignation. ''I'm not the least interested in your exhibit number one, or whatever you want to call it.''

A corner of his mouth curled into the barest of smiles. ''I see. Then, to what do I owe the pleasure of your visit?''

She assessed him coolly. Now shaven, his face was the one in the searing images in her memory. But she couldn't deny that it was a handsome face. The only noticeable change seemed to be that his dark hair, which fell in disarray across his forehead, was shot through with silver, particularly at the temples. ''I've come to apologize,'' she said finally.

He stepped back from the door. "Please, come in and sit down."

Erin stepped across the black-and-white tiles of a hallway that was once filled with the rainbow glow of Mrs. Swayze's stained-glass lamp and a collection of "welcome" signs. Only now, the hall was stripped bare.

In the living room, a rug that Erin recognized as an expensive Persian lay on the floor amid unopened packing boxes. Almost everything appeared to be where the movers left it—a sofa here, an armchair there, a lamp on the floor. She sat on the edge of the sofa, setting the basket at her feet. Wyatt took the chair, easing into it gingerly.

"Little Lily leaves a lasting impression," he said, his eyes clouded with pain.

Erin felt a pang of guilt. "I'm terribly sorry. She will want to apologize personally. I'll bring her over."

He quickly thrust his palm into the air. "Please, that's not necessary."

She shot him a wounded look.

His eyes narrowed. "You think I'm an ogre, don't you?"

Erin responded with a chilly silence.

As he shifted his weight, he winced, almost imperceptibly. "Erin, would you mind telling me what I've done wrong here?"

"Don't act so innocent," she said crossly.

His jaw stiffened. "In the last two days, I've had my house invaded by an unsupervised child, my lunch eaten by your dog, hours of work dropped into a bucket of water, and my spine misaligned by a stray crayon. And you act as if the big bad wolf has moved in next door to three defenseless little pigs."

A surge of anger arced through her like electricity. "On behalf of myself and the two other little pigs, I'm heartily sorry for having caused you pain and suffering. But it will never hurt as much as the things you said about me in that courtroom. And don't tell me it was just legal theatrics. You believed those things you said, and it's apparent that you still do. You can't deny that.''

He responded with a silence that seemed to chill the entire room.

Erin rose. ''I'm not naive, Wyatt Keegan. There's more than just a coincidence that you've taken up residence next door. I don't trust you.''

Wyatt stood, his color deepening. ''Listen to me,'' he said, taking her by the shoulders.

She twisted away from him, but his grip remained firm. The heat of his strong fingers burned through the soft cotton of her T-shirt.

''Look at me, Erin,'' he demanded.

Her eyes turned to his. For an instant, she was almost lost in their depths.

''You're wrong about me,'' he said.

''What do you know about the bond between a parent, or guardian, and a child?'' she asked.

His eyes took on a pained and troubled look but he said nothing. His arms dropped from her shoulders and he stepped back, his jaw set firmly.

She sensed she'd inadvertently struck a vein of raw feeling. ''Did I say something terribly wrong?''

''Let's make a deal,'' he said, ignoring the question. His voice was tight. ''Let's arrange some sort of détente here. I won't bother you and Lily if you won't bother me. Let's aim for a peaceful coexistence. Is that fair enough?''

Erin studied him warily. The proposal sounded reasonable, almost too reasonable. ''You could always move, you know. How about a house on the mountaintop? You could surround yourself with a spiked fence, a moat, and snarling dogs.''

A glint of mirth appeared in his eyes. His amusement only served to deepen Erin's anger.

''I'm content to stay here as long as we can stay on our respective sides of the fence,'' he said. ''Shall we agree to that?''

''Do you want it in writing?'' she asked sardonically.

''I'll settle for a handshake.'' He offered a large, square hand.

After a slight hesitation, she slipped her hand into his. The warmth and strength of his touch brought an unwanted flutter to her heart. In dismay, she pulled back.

''Good-bye,'' she said stiffly, turning away.

''Wait,'' he said. ''You've forgotten your basket.''

She picked it up off the carpet and handed it to him. ''It's for you.'' Her words were underscored with irony. ''Welcome to the neighborhood.''

Chapter Three

Their coexistence was outwardly peaceful, but within, Erin wasn't at peace at all. She'd instructed Lily to be on her best behavior and not to leave the yard without permission. She'd told herself to stop worrying about Wyatt Keegan. But his presence next door was a looming one, even though they were separated by an expanse of lawn and a white picket fence.

It was obvious he still thought the judge had made a mistake in awarding her guardianship of Lily. Lily was spirited, to be sure. But Erin feared that the word lurking in Wyatt's mind was more like "unruly." The child needed, he'd said, his strong baritone filling the courtroom, a normal, orderly existence; two parents, not one; parents of means.

But Lily wouldn't have known that with her own parents. Her father and mother had given her a wealth of love and attention, but they'd died with only seventy-six dollars in the bank. And it must be obvious to Wyatt that Erin wasn't much better off, she thought, with a sinking feeling. Hadn't she depleted her savings fighting for Lily?

She prepared an order for an antique Swedish hand-painted trunk. A decorator in New Hampshire had asked her to initiate a search for a fussy client of Swedish descent, someone named Forsythia, who didn't care how many kronas it cost. Only a trunk imported directly from Sweden would do. But as she prepared a fax to send to a Swedish contact, her thoughts strayed again. She had to show Wyatt Keegan that he was wrong about herself and Lily, that she was a perfectly sensible person and that Lily was no wild child.

He'd see that, until he came to town, theirs had been a stable, orderly existence. Without permission, Lily would never set another sneaker on his lawn. The bungalow, by all outward appearances, would become the very essence of order, peace, and tranquillity. Wyatt Keegan would be soundly proven wrong, she thought with satisfaction.

For three days, there was hardly a sign of him, just an occasional thump of a car door closing or a rectangle of yellow light from a window at night. But on the fourth, a Saturday morning, she found a brown paper bag next to the front door. It was neatly tied with twine. Inside was the lasagna dish, sparkling clean. It contained a note, written with black ink in a bold, masculine scrawl.

"In accordance with our pact, I won't disturb you. But the lasagna was excellent, and I'll think about it with pleasure as I stumble about in my own kitchen. Many thanks. Your partner in détente, Wyatt."

Erin twisted a corner of her mouth as she read the note again. So he really means this, she thought. Well, she would certainly stay out of his way and make sure that Lily did as well.

Almost having forgotten why she stepped out onto the porch in the first place, she scooped the newspaper up off the top step and gave Wyatt's house a sidelong glance. The BMW gleamed in the driveway; every blade of grass seemed perfectly in place. A normal, orderly existence, she thought with a twinge of annoyance.

Almost as if orchestrated to go with her thoughts, a rumble of thunder sounded in the distance. She looked up to find a gray flannel sky and a menacing stillness in the air. A spit of moisture touched her cheek.

She quickly stepped back inside where Lily sat cross-legged on one of the worn Turkish carpets watching Saturday morning cartoons. Wiggles lay beside her, chewing a toy bone.

"What is that?" Lily asked, eyeing the package.

"Mr. Keegan returned the lasagna dish."

"Am I still not 'lowed to go to his house anymore?"

"Not unless you're invited," Erin said.

"Can I ask him to invite me?"

Erin smiled ruefully. "No, honey. It doesn't work that way. You have to wait to be asked."

"Oh," she said, her chin dropping.

Erin felt a pang of remorse, followed by a little spark of anger. Perhaps she couldn't fault Wyatt for being annoyed over Lily's unintentional mischief, but was he going to hold it against her forever? She knelt down and brushed a stray tendril of dark hair from the child's cheek. And that look on his face when she'd asked if he knew anything about a parent-child bond. Why would such a question seem to disturb him so much?

"I don't want him to be mad at me," the little girl said.

Erin felt a little ache. "If he is, I'm sure he won't be for very long," she said, trying to convince herself as well. "It's just that some people are unaccustomed to children. Come on," she said, giving her voice a lightness she didn't feel, "let's have some waffles."

Waffles were a Saturday morning tradition. Sometimes, Erin tossed chocolate chips into the batter, sometimes chopped nuts. As she waited in the kitchen for the waffle iron to heat, a loud crack of thunder rattled the windows, sending her heart into her throat. Lily, openmouthed, clamped her hands over her ears as Wiggles scurried under her chair. Then the sky unleashed a curtain of rain.

Lily scrambled to the window, leaning into the sill. "Rain, rain, go away. Come again another day," she shouted at the torrent. Then she coaxed Wiggles from under the chair, hugged him, and cooed reassuringly: "I'll protect you."

A smile touched Erin's lips. This was the Lily that Wyatt Keegan needed to see.

"How come it doesn't thunder when it snows?" Lily asked contemplatively, as they ate their breakfast.

Erin pursed her lips in thought.

"How come?" Lily persisted.

"I don't know," Erin replied. "Maybe we can call up the weatherman and ask."

"Maybe Mr. Keegan knows," Lily suggested, pushing her mostly empty plate away.

"It's not likely," Erin said with a twinge of concern. Despite everything that had happened, the little girl seemed intrigued with the man. "It's time to brush your teeth," she said, quickly changing the subject.

Lily scrambled from her chair and trudged toward the bathroom.

Erin was clearing the table when she heard Lily running back toward the kitchen. "Aunt Erin!" she cried. "It's raining in the house!"

She set the plates down with a rattle and tore out of the kitchen. She found Lily standing in the dining room watching a puddle spread on the oak floor. Above, a steady trickle came from the ceiling. Her stomach somersaulted.

"Get some towels from the bathroom. I'll get a bucket,"

she said, trying to keep her voice even. But the instant the child left the room, Erin clamped her hands over her head in exasperation. In the spring, the bathroom ceiling had sprung a leak. Now, it was the dining room again. Much more of this and the house would be taking on water like the *Titanic*. And she'd been counting on the Didier account to help replace the roof.

She sighed deeply. There was nothing to do but what she did the last time—patch it herself.

Lily came back into the room dragging a pile of towels which Erin laid over the puddle. After the water was mopped up, Erin placed a bucket under the leak.

She had to empty it once before it finally stopped raining. By early afternoon, the sun was shining through the thinning clouds. Seizing the opportunity, Erin hurried to the garage and dragged out the ladder. With a struggle, she raised it up to the eaves.

"Promise to stay right there where I can see you," she told Lily, pointing to a grassy area bordering the fence. She'd set out a patio chair and a puzzle for her. Wiggles, confined to the backyard, yapped unhappily.

"I promise I won't bother Mr. Keegan," she said. "I'll be good."

"I know you will, sweetheart," she said. She frowned as her gaze swept over his normal, orderly house. His car sat in his normal, orderly driveway, but that was the only hint that someone might be inside the house. And she hoped he would stay there and mind his normal, orderly business.

With a spare but mismatched shingle in one hand and the other firmly gripping the rail of the ladder, Erin climbed slowly upward. A putty knife, a hammer, a small can of roofing compound, and some roofing nails jingled in the large pocket on the front of her apron. Now at eye level with the gutter, she turned to check on Lily. The child, apparently accustomed by now to seeing Erin on the roof, was now doll-sized and absorbed in her game.

Erin set the patching compound on the gutter and carefully surveyed the aged and curling shingles. Near the spot where she guessed the dining-room leak to be, a shingle was torn, apparently snapped off by the wind. She carefully hoisted herself from the top rung of the ladder to the eave. She plucked the can of patching compound from the gutter and scooted backwards up the roof. Granules from the worn and brittle shingles crunched under her feet.

Finally situated next to the leak, she pried the old shingle off, laid a thick layer of compound on the spot, and placed a new shingle over it. She stopped and stared at it as if daring the roof to leak again.

She slapped the lid back on the can and tucked it into her apron. With the granules on the shingles biting into her palms, she inched her way toward the ladder. She'd positioned her foot on the first rung and was beginning the climb down when the ladder suddenly slid to one side, pitching her off balance. She clutched wildly at the rails of the ladder but they were no longer there. Her heart seemed to lunge from her chest as she tumbled toward the ground in a blur.

She landed with a dull splat, only vaguely aware that the ladder had slammed into the soggy ground only inches away.

It was Lily's cries that brought her back to her senses.

"Aunt Erin! Aunt Erin!" The little girl's arms flew around her neck. "Are you broken?"

Before she could answer, Wyatt suddenly flashed into

view, coming at her in a full run and sprinting over the three-foot fence separating their yards.

He halted in a kneeling position at her feet. "Are you okay?" he asked breathlessly.

Erin dully felt her legs, then her arms, and made a clumsy attempt to get up. "I'm perfectly fine," she said, trying to recoup her dignity. There was a hint of defiance in her voice.

He caught her by the arm. "Take it easy, now." His strong fingers sent an unwanted current of heat through her.

"Thank you, Wyatt, but I can manage," she said, trying to get up under her own power.

This time he caught her by both arms and held her in place. "Don't be so sure."

Her gaze burned into his clear, dark eyes. "Don't be so unsure."

The corners of his well-sculpted mouth tightened. "You didn't get the sass knocked out of you, did you?"

"Would you let me get up, please?" she asked, ignoring his question.

He gave her a chiding look, then released his hold on her. He stood back with his hands on his hips and gazed at her skeptically from under furrowed brows.

Erin, feeling a growing soreness, rose unsteadily, trying not to wince. Lily rushed up and threw her little arms around her hips. "Poor Aunt Erin. I'll get you a Band-Aid."

"Thank you, but that won't be necessary," she said, greatly minimizing her smarting bruises. "I'll be all right."

Erin glanced up to see Wyatt watching them intently. Her eyes met his for an instant, causing her heart to skip a beat. He quickly turned away and an awkward silence followed. It was broken finally by a bark from the Yorkie.

Erin stroked the child's sleek, glossy hair. ''Why don't you go check on Wiggles?''

The little girl set off running toward the backyard, her hair flying.

Wyatt looked at Erin with narrowed eyes. ''What are you doing risking life and limb like that?'' he demanded once Lily was out of sight.

''What were you doing watching me?'' she countered, her cheeks warm with indignation.

''There wasn't anything interesting on TV,'' he said drolly.

She shot him a look of pure annoyance. ''I'm happy to have provided your afternoon entertainment.''

His chin crinkled. ''I would have helped, but by the time I noticed your little ballet on the roof, you were executing some odd little arabesque toward the ground.''

''I didn't need any help,'' she said defensively.

''The evidence indicates otherwise,'' he said, eyeing the fallen ladder.

Erin looked at him through narrowed eyes. ''It's a low roof. Otherwise, I would have never gotten up there. I survived, didn't I?''

''Through sheer luck,'' he argued. ''You shouldn't be doing this yourself, Erin. It's too dangerous. You've got a child to take care of.''

Her cheeks burned hotly, but she said nothing. She couldn't argue against reason. Yet she didn't want to admit to him that she couldn't afford to have the roof properly repaired.

''I'll be happy to help with your next project,'' he said, rolling his sleeves up over muscular forearms. ''Just ask and I'll be at your service.''

Erin looked at him skeptically. ''Thank you, but I suspect your construction skills are even more limited than mine. You've probably had more experience holding a gold-plated fountain pen than a hammer.''

A small dimple appeared in his cheek. ''I *do* know how to hold a ladder.''

Erin folded her arms across her chest. ''Didn't we agree to stay out of each other's hair? Isn't that what détente means?''

''Yes, to both questions,'' he said.

Erin looked at him smugly. ''Well?''

Ignoring her, he shoved his hands deeply into his pockets and strolled closer to the house. He looked up at the eaves, then down at the ground where the imprints of the legs of the ladder remained. ''The ground was too soggy to support a ladder,'' he said. ''It could have been a lot more than your pride that was wounded. Instead of telling me to mind my own business, you should be thankful that I wasn't.''

The sting of his words made her more resentful than grateful. But in a show of dignity, she straightened her small frame, mindful that the slightest movement caused an ache here and a pain there. ''Thank you,'' she said. ''I don't know how I've managed without you all these years.''

The barest glint of a smile appeared on his lips, making Erin even more furious. His chin was perfectly square, his nose perfectly straight. Even the strand of sable hair which had fallen across his forehead was perfectly distracting. He was smug, arrogant, self-assured, and all too thoroughly confident, she thought, bristling. The words clicked through her mind like a thesaurus, but none carded the punch she wanted to deliver to his perfect nose. Instead, she bit her tongue.

"You should get a look at yourself in the mirror," he said smoothly.

"Why?" she retorted "I know what I look like."

Undaunted by the ring of belligerence in her voice, he took a step toward her and placed his fingers beneath her chin, sending a ripple of sensation along her spine. She turned her face away from him, but not before his thumb swept over her cheek, faintly touching her lower lip. She jerked back as if his hand were a plume of flame.

He held up a thumb streaked with mud. "Actually, it was rather becoming," he said, his gaze sweeping over her.

Before she could reply, Lily burst through the backyard gate, followed by Wiggles. The dog wore a black T-shirt with "Killer" in white letters across the chest. On his head was a little pink straw sombrero held in place by an elastic chin strap. He stopped within a few feet of their visitor and began barking furiously.

Wyatt blinked.

Erin knelt quickly to hush the dog, but when she did, the sudden movement sent a flash of pain across her knee. Clamping a hand on it, she let out a soft moan.

Wyatt touched her shoulder gently. She wished he'd quit touching her. At the same time, she wished he wouldn't. "Are you all right? Perhaps it would be a good idea for you to see a doctor."

Erin shook her head adamantly. "I'll be fine."

One of his brows rose skeptically.

She patted the dog on the sombrero and rose slowly. "He's very protective," she explained.

Wyatt glanced at Wiggles, then her. "It's very reassuring that you and Lily have such a mighty beast to keep you out of harm's way."

"He can bite," Lily interjected.

Wyatt looked down at the small dog who was panting happily, his hat now askew. "I'm terrified," he said flatly.

"He won't act mean if he knows you," Lily said brightly. "I know." She suddenly bounced on her toes. "You can come to my house and play with him. We can have a tea party."

Wyatt swallowed hard.

Erin's stomach tightened. "Honey, it's very nice of you to ask, but Mr. Keegan is very busy."

The child's face fell.

Wyatt cleared his throat. "I'd be very happy to come," he said, turning his gaze toward Erin. His expression was oddly somber. "That is, if it's all right with your Aunt Erin."

Erin froze. Wyatt's eyes were laden with expectation, as if he were daring her to refuse. So much for détente. After the tea party, she'd hope that he'd stay on his side of the fence. But in the meantime, for Lily's sake, she'd pretend they were friends.

"Of course," she said in her most gracious tone. "Lily would enjoy it so much."

"I'll look forward to it," he said.

Erin tried to ignore the hint of mischief in his eyes. "How is three o'clock on Sunday afternoon?"

He smiled mysteriously. "I wouldn't miss it."

Erin gnawed at the inside of her cheek as she polished the child-sized table in Lily's room. Wyatt had a knack for seeing them at their lesser moments. Now he'd seen her tumble off a leaky roof. She hardly looked like a woman in control, she thought worriedly, attacking the painted planks with circular motions.

She laid a crisp white doily on the table. Later, she'd

add a vase as a centerpiece. Lily had been sent to the backyard for a bunch of daisies to fill it.

The little table was surrounded by four small but mismatched chairs. Lily's teddy bear sat in one, his button eyes staring blankly ahead and his stomach threadbare. Erin stood back and quickly surveyed the room. The walls were yellow, the woodwork blue. The small iron bed was painted purple. Vines grew from a window box and up over a trellis framing the window. A red-and-white polka-dotted swing, secured to the rafters by ropes, hung from the ceiling. Trees were painted on the walls, giving it the look of a forest. Today, it was a carefully tidied forest.

The tea party would be Lily's second. The first was inspired when Erin came across a rose-patterned English teapot with matching cups and saucers. Thinking it would also be an opportunity to teach Lily some old-fashioned social graces, she invited Tabitha Penobscot's grand-nieces. The occasion was such a success that Lily had been anxious to repeat it. It wasn't that Lily cared about social niceties; she simply enjoyed having company.

Nevertheless, Erin taught her some hostess lines: "I'm happy you could come to my party." "Please have some cookies." "I had a good time. I hope you had a good time, too." Despite what Wyatt Keegan thought, she knew something about how to raise a mannerly and considerate child.

Her thoughts were interrupted by the slam of the back door and the sound of hurried footsteps. "The vase is in the kitchen," Erin called, stepping into the hallway.

Lily, her dark hair gleaming, was a show-stopper in a pink dress with puffed sleeves and a lace-trimmed collar that Erin had discovered in a secondhand shop. A sash was tied into a large bow at the back, making her look like such a perfect little lady that it brought a lump to Erin's throat.

But when the doorbell rang, the child dropped her flower basket inside the kitchen door and took off running, sash flying, like a Little Leaguer tearing toward home base.

Erin's heart kicked. "Slow down," she admonished in a loud whisper.

But the call was barely heeded. With Wiggles at her heels, she gave the doorknob a twist with both hands and pulled the door open. Wyatt's broad-shouldered form appeared. Erin's blood surged.

"Good afternoon, Lily."

Wiggles growled softly, but Lily hushed him with a quick pat. "Hi, Mr. Keegan. I'm happy you could come to my party."

Erin's heart warmed with pride as she made her way to the door.

"Please come in," she said.

Wyatt glanced at her with a hint of amusement. "How nice of Lily to invite me."

Erin ignored the obvious reference to the single invitation. She also tried to ignore how handsome he looked in a dark gray suit and crisp white shirt. The knot of his teal blue print tie was slightly askew at his throat. Erin was horrified at her fleeting impulse to straighten it.

"Mr. Keegan is wearing his party clothes, too," Lily observed with obvious pleasure.

"You," he said, bending his tall frame slightly, "look very pretty in yours."

"Thank you," she said.

"Please, call me Wyatt," he said.

"Yes, sir," she replied.

Lily's perfect manners and appearance gave Erin a sense of defiant pride. But her admiring gaze halted abruptly at the child's feet. Instead of her black patent party shoes, Lily wore a pair of dirty and worn blue-and-white sneakers. One shoelace was untied. Erin gulped.

Wyatt produced a small cellophane bag tied with a bright red bow. It was filled with dog biscuits. "Perhaps Wiggles will like these."

The dog sniffed at the air. "Wiggles likes it when you give him food," Lily said.

Wyatt gave the bow a quick yank and held a bone-shaped treat slightly over Wiggles's head. With a quick snap, the dog took it between his teeth and trotted off.

Lily grinned.

"Would you make sure the table is ready?" Erin asked. "Did you remember the flowers?"

Lily clamped a hand over her mouth and darted off toward the kitchen.

"You really didn't have to bring anything," Erin said, taking the package of treats.

Wyatt shrugged his square shoulders. "I'd planned to bring over a bunch of zinnias from my yard, but they seemed to have vanished in the aftermath of the storm."

"It did make a mess of things," she acknowledged.

"You included," he reminded her.

She gave him a scolding look.

"You're all right now?" His tone was surprisingly gentle.

"Just a few bruises and a scraped knee. Why don't you join us in Lily's room?" she asked, eager to change the subject.

As she turned to leave, he touched her shoulder. "Erin." There was a short pause. "I know we agreed to maintain a civil distance. I'm more than willing to do that. But there's a third person in this equation. I'm here because I didn't want to hurt Lily's feelings. You understand, don't you?''

Erin felt an inexplicable little pang from somewhere underneath her heart. ''Of course.''

''I'm afraid I've already been a little too stern with her and . . .'' He took a deep breath. ''I'm sorry.''

Erin bit her lower lip. ''I should apologize, too. I know you were just trying to be helpful yesterday when I fell. As for Lily, I should realize that not everyone has unlimited patience for children.''

Wyatt swallowed hard. ''Erin, I . . . I do know something about the parent-child bond. I was a father—almost. My wife was killed in an accident when she was five months pregnant.''

Erin turned cold. ''I'm so sorry.''

He touched her arm as if to keep her from going on. ''It's not anything I want to talk about. I know you understand.''

Before Erin could respond further, Lily burst into the room. She grabbed Wyatt's fingers and gave them a tug. ''Come in my room,'' she said. ''I got everything all ready.''

''Lily's tea parlor,'' Erin explained.

Wyatt nodded stiffly as the child took the lead. He adjusted his long strides to Lily's skipping. Erin followed, still reeling from what he'd just told her. Dealing with her and Lily had to be doubly difficult for him. They were surely unpleasant reminders of what he'd lost.

When they entered the room, Wiggles got up from his basket at the foot of Lily's bed. He eyed Wyatt warily but made no sound.

''He didn't bark,'' Lily announced brightly. ''See, I told you.''

"Indeed you did," Wyatt said. "If only all disputes could be settled so easily."

Erin could feel his eyes on her but she looked down to avoid his gaze. It was then that she noticed the riot of zinnias at the center of the little table. Her breath caught. She glanced at Wyatt to find his eyes riveted as well to the bouquet. Their eyes met for an instant, his brightening with amusement. Erin's cheeks flamed.

"Perhaps we can talk later," she whispered, swallowing hard.

A hint of a smile appeared on his lips, but he said nothing.

Lily stood proudly at the table which was already set with the rose-patterned cups and saucers and pink glass dessert plates.

"Please sit down," Lily said in a rehearsed tone. She placed a hand on a small chair.

Wyatt's eyes widened. "I'm afraid . . ."

"Don't worry," Erin interjected. "They're very strong." Finally, it was her turn to be amused, but the moment was dimmed by the presence of the zinnias on the table.

A dimple of skepticism appeared in his chin. But he gingerly lowered his large frame into the little chair. His knees, once he was seated, were almost even with his chest. He looked askance at the teddy bear seated next to him, then gave Erin a slow smile, one that melted her resistance so quickly that it alarmed her.

"If you'll excuse me, I'll get the tea," she said, her voice tight, and quickly turned away.

In the kitchen, she accidentally overfilled the tea kettle and dropped one of the Russian tea cakes she'd baked that morning. Her nerves danced wildly as she waited for the water to boil. She didn't understand it. Lily knew not to take things that belonged to others.

But regardless of all that, there was yet another undercurrent of anxiety. Wyatt's presence disturbed her on two levels. His dark good looks distracted her. And could a man who could sit good-naturedly through a child's tea party be all that bad, especially when he couldn't help but remember the child he'd lost? Torn by conflicting thoughts, Erin dropped a ball of herbal tea into the pot and willed it to steep quickly. Wyatt Keegan couldn't leave soon enough—for her sake and his own.

She set the cookies and teapot on a French tole-painted tray. As she approached Lily's room, she could hear the child chattering brightly. How quickly children forget life's little squabbles, Erin mused.

Wyatt shifted carefully in the little chair, but his attention remained tightly focused on Lily. He hardly seemed to notice Erin entering the room.

"I can count backwards, too. Want to hear me?" she asked him. Without waiting for a response, she began, "Ten, nine . . ."

Erin felt a fleeting moment of satisfaction. Perhaps she hadn't convinced Wyatt that Lily was getting the best upbringing possible, but Lily herself, however unwittingly, was putting on a good show.

"Let's have some tea and cookies," Erin interrupted gently, giving Wyatt a quick but knowing glance.

"After our tea, I can sing you the alphabet song," Lily offered.

Wyatt glanced at Erin. "I like a woman who's never at a loss for words."

Erin gave him a look of mock impatience and filled his cup. Lily placed a tea cake on his plate, licked the powdered sugar off her fingers, then added a second, on which she'd left damp fingerprints.

Erin, trying hard to conceal a smile, took a seat on the other side of the teddy bear. But when Lily got up to coax Wiggles to the table, Erin, using silver-plated tongs, quickly put the cookie on her own plate and replaced it with a fresh one, ignoring Wyatt's gestures of protest.

Lily handed Wiggles a dog biscuit that she'd laid on one of the dessert plates. With a smudge of powdered sugar on her cheek, she smiled sweetly at Wyatt. "You took your mask off."

Wyatt's lips broadened into a smile as he stroked a closely shaven jaw. "I decided the country look wasn't really me."

Lily reached over and touched his cheek.

Erin shifted uncomfortably in her chair. "She's unaccustomed to male visitors," she explained briefly.

"Just Ronald and Caleb and Ralph," Lily added innocently.

"I see," he said, raising a winglike eyebrow.

Her stomach tightened. "They're just . . ."

"Friends?" he finished, looking at her with interest.

"Yes, but they also fix things and . . ." Erin felt herself sinking into verbal quicksand. No matter if she explained that Ronald was the mailman, Caleb was Tabitha Penobscot's son and Ralph was the plumber, he'd still wonder. After all, where were they when the roof needed fixing?

Wyatt turned to Lily.

"I've had a wonderful time," he said, setting down his teacup. "You've been a most gracious hostess and you and your aunt and Wiggles have been very nice company."

The little girl beamed.

"But now," he continued, "I'm afraid I have to go."

Lily frowned. ''But do you have to?''

''I have to have some work ready in the morning for a client.''

Lily got up and placed her arms around Wyatt's neck.

His outstretched arms froze momentarily as if he didn't know what to do with them. Then slowly, he embraced the child. As he did, Erin was struck by the eclipse of light in his eyes. He pulled Lily gently away and stood up.

''What's a plient?'' Lily asked.

''A client is someone that you do work for,'' he explained, his voice tight. ''In this case, it's someone you know—your aunt and uncle in Boston.''

Erin's nerves crackled.

He looked at Erin through narrowed eyes. ''It's the Holbrookes.''

Chapter Four

Erin set her teacup down with a rattle. She touched a linen napkin to her lips before trusting her voice. "Yes, of course, Lily remembers. They send gifts at Christmas and on her birthday."

For Lily's sake, she always spoke well of the Holbrookes, but underneath was a lingering undercurrent of anger. They seemed to want to maintain a connection to the little girl, but only once in the two years that Erin had become her permanent guardian had the couple visited her. And then, she had been too young to understand who they were. What Lily needed, Erin thought, was not expensive gifts, but their time, love, and attention.

"They're doing well?" Erin asked as pleasantly as she could.

Wyatt fingered the knot in his tie. "Yes. Yale is buying another company, one of his competitors'. I'm doing some of the legal work."

"He was always quite the businessman," Erin responded, trying to push back the associations it brought. Yale had never understood his brother-in-law's commitment to the art of pottery making and the poor earnings potential that came with it.

"Yes, very much so," Wyatt said, his voice tight. His eyes met hers in a glint of shared memories that extended to the contention in the courtroom. As an awkward silence descended over the room, Erin glanced quickly away, at Lily. Seemingly having grown bored with the adults' conversation, she was poking an index finger into the traces of powdered sugar on her plate and touching her finger to her tongue. At that moment, Wiggles jumped up into Wyatt's chair and began licking his plate.

"Oh, Wiggles," Erin groaned, grabbing the dog and putting him on her lap.

Lily muffled a giggle with her hand.

Wyatt smiled wryly, bringing a dimple to his cheek. "Every moment seems to be an adventure here."

"It's a zoo," Lily exclaimed.

Erin blinked at the child in surprise. That was somewhat of an exaggeration, and where in all of Vermont had she picked up that expression?

"Well, sometimes, maybe," Erin said, quickly moving in to put things in their proper perspective.

Wyatt, slightly lifting one perfect, black eyebrow, appeared somewhat unconvinced.

"Hardly ever," she said defensively, holding Wiggles to her chest.

Wyatt's gaze swept from her face to her shoulder. With Wiggles fidgeting in her arms, the strap of her navy-and-white checked sundress had slipped and his eyes lingered appreciatively on her bare, lightly tanned shoulder. Erin quickly set the dog down, slipped the strap up, and shot Wyatt a look of warning.

The corners of his mouth twitched upward into an almost imperceptible smile. He rose and looked down at Lily, who was gazing up at him admiringly.

"It was a very nice tea party, Lily," he said, leaning down and placing his hands on his knees. "I must say again that you're a charming hostess. Thank you for inviting me."

"Thank you for coming to my party," Lily said, delivering the line without a cue.

Wiggles playfully circled Wyatt's perfectly shined shoes. "See, he likes you," the child exclaimed.

Wyatt grinned crookedly. "That's two out of three," he said, glancing at Erin. "I suppose that's not too bad."

Erin ignored the remark, but she wasn't so successful in ignoring his smile. It was a disarming smile, she acknowledged with alarm. He never hinted at being able to perform such a common physical feat while he was pacing back and forth in front of the judge. Then, that well-chiseled face seemed to be made of titanium.

"It was very nice of you to come," she said, hiding behind a veneer of formality.

"My pleasure," he said, touching Lily's glossy crown.

Erin, followed by a skipping Lily and a trotting Wiggles, accompanied him to the front door.

" 'Bye, Wyatt," the child called, waving from the front porch as he strode down the sidewalk.

Erin watched as he waved back, the summer breeze ruffling his dark hair. Then, with hurried strides, he was gone. But Erin's sense of relief over his departure was brief and fleeting.

Taking Lily by the hand, she took her inside. "Lily," she said in a half whisper, "where did the zinnias come from?"

"From the Swayzes," she said innocently.

Erin's heart sank. "But sweetheart, you weren't supposed to go over there."

"But I didn't," she insisted.

"How did you get them?"

"I'll show you."

Lily led her into the backyard to the picket fence separating their yard from Wyatt's. She pointed to a cluster of plucked stems sticking through the pickets. She knelt down and slipped her hand through one of the gaps in the fence and picked off a piece of foliage from the other side. "See, Aunt Erin? I didn't go over there. I minded you."

Erin inwardly groaned. "Lily, those aren't our flowers."

The child looked confused. "But Mrs. Swayze said I could have some. We planted them together."

She bent to the child's level. "They're Wyatt's now. I'm afraid he thinks you've come in his yard and taken his flowers without permission."

"I'll give them back," she said earnestly.

"Maybe we should. We can put a note with them, explaining how you got them. We wouldn't want him to think we've been in his yard picking his flowers, would we?"

"No," she murmured.

"That's a good girl," Erin said, giving her another hug. It pained her to cause Lily to fret but she didn't want a very particular man next door getting the wrong impression of a sweet and obedient child.

Later, as Erin put together Lily's favorite dish of homemade macaroni and cheese, Wyatt's presence seemed to linger in the house. She wanted to break free of the painful memories of the past but, because of him, she couldn't.

Erin added another layer of cheese to the top of the casserole as Lily drew a picture to send to Wyatt along with the bouquet of flowers. There was also the matter of the ruined computer disk, and she wasn't quite sure what to do about that. It was much more than just replacing the disk. There were the hours of time that Wyatt had lost. Perhaps she could do some timesaving chore for him, such as raking leaves. With a yard dotted with maples, he'd have leaves practically up to his windowsills. She wanted him to think well of herself and Lily, especially considering his continuing association with the Holbrookes. She certainly didn't want to give Wyatt or the Holbrookes any more reasons to believe that Lily was in the wrong hands.

The next morning, just as soon as Erma McCosky, mother of nine and Maple Springs's highest-mileage carpooler, picked Lily up for preschool, Erin rushed up to Main Street to pick up a couple of six-inch pots of yellow chrysanthemums. She figured that, in addition to the zinnias, that should make it more than even as far as their flower debt to Wyatt Keegan was concerned.

She returned a half hour later with the flowers in the trunk of her aging little car.

Until Wyatt arrived, it hardly mattered that she had the oldest car and the most weather-beaten house on the block. But much to her annoyance, she was sure it hadn't escaped his notice. She ran inside the house, grabbed the zinnias, which she'd set aside in a fruit jar wrapped with green tissue paper and a twine bow, and placed them on the little brick stoop outside his door. She placed the mums next to it, along with a drawing from Lily and a note from herself.

''Sorry,'' she'd written, ''but the wind pushed the zinnias through the fence and Lily harvested the rest by reaching through a hole. Since she and Mrs. Swayze planted them, she thought they were hers as well. Please, accept our apologies, along with some mums and Lily's picture of a blue zinnia. Signed: Erin, Lily, and Wiggles March.'' Lily had insisted that Wiggles's name be added.

That evening, there was no sign of Wyatt until nine o'clock, just after Lily had been put to bed. As she left the little girl's room after reading her a story, Erin caught the flash of headlights in her living-room window as the car pulled into the driveway. Watching from the darkened room, she saw his tall silhouette bend down in front of his door. A moment later, squares of light appeared in his living-room windows.

Erin stepped back. It was probably a first for this proper Bostonian—receiving a note from, among others, a Yorkshire terrier. In addition to the proverbial silver spoon, he'd probably been born with a suit and tie, taught to mind his manners, not to get his clothes dirty, and keep his fingers off the antiques. And then he meets the free-spirited, overall-clad Lily, Erin mused. Now that the Little Prince had met Huckleberry Finn, he'd probably never be the same.

The next day, there wasn't a squeak out of Wyatt; not that Erin expected one. But on the second morning, when she stepped out to pick up the newspaper, she found the mums, along with three more pots of them, clustered by the front door. Her heart kicked, in surprise. Erin reached for a small envelope tucked in the leaves of one of the plants. She opened it to find a brief note written in a bold, masculine scrawl of black ink.

"Some years ago, there was a Mrs. Roosevelt whose jonquils were plucked bare by a small boy named Wyatt Keegan.

"As for Lily, no harm done. These mums are for her, along with my appreciation for being her guest at her lovely party.

"Yours, in continued détente, Wyatt."

Erin's spirits took an upward leap, then faltered like a kite in a fickle wind. Lily would be delighted with his response, but the last line was a not-so-subtle reminder that they were supposed to be keeping a polite distance from each other. The party—in this case, Lily's—was over.

Erin felt vaguely empty as she stepped back inside. She should be ecstatic that he wanted to stay over there and mind his own business. But she had an odd, nagging regret about it, because for a moment, when he cared enough to come to a little girl's tea party, and she saw his handsome smile for the first time, he'd become harder to dislike.

They'd transferred the flowers to two large clay pots and put them on each side of the front door. The cooler September weather suited them and they bloomed luxuriantly, forming plump, golden cushions. But while the flowers were hard to miss, Wyatt was hard to spot. He often left early and came home late. And when they did see him, he offered only a restrained greeting and a wave.

But Lily's interest in his comings and goings didn't wane. She reported to Erin when the mail carrier left him a package or when he had pizza delivered.

Erin grew more concerned that Lily and Wiggles might somehow end up at Wyatt's house again, wreaking yet more havoc. But most of all, Erin was concerned that Lily was beginning to like the man. Who knew what he could have up his crisply starched, white pinpoint oxford sleeve?

What she and Lily needed was a distraction. The following weekend, one presented itself—the Maple County Fair.

Lily talked excitedly of it for days, losing some of her interest in anything going on at the saltbox house next door, much to Erin's satisfaction.

"We don't have a lot of money to spend because I'm saving to fix the roof," she explained to Lily, "but we can go on a couple of rides and get a candy apple."

"I got two nickels," Lily offered.

Erin smiled. "You're a sweetheart, but I think we can manage without them."

Saturday afternoon was clear and crisp, perfect for fair-going. The leaves were beginning to show their first hints of color but were no match for Lily, who was outfitted in denim overalls, a taxi yellow turtleneck, and her red high-top sneakers. She wore a purple teddy bear backpack containing a comb, a storybook, and a small box of juice.

Erin, dressed in jeans, sneakers, and wearing a long-sleeved red T-shirt, caught sight of the BMW in Wyatt's driveway as she stepped off the front porch and started toward the car. But there was no sign of its owner.

She quickly strapped Lily to the front seat of the Escort and slipped behind the steering wheel. ''We're ready to blast off to the fair. Do the countdown, Lily.''

Lily leaned forward excitedly and counted backwards from ten, not missing a number. Erin ceremoniously stuck the key into the ignition and gave it a quick twist, but nothing happened.

She felt a dull jolt of surprise. She turned the key again, this time getting only a weak bleat. Her heartbeat quickened. She tried it again, then again, managing hardly more than a warble from the engine.

''Oh, no,'' she said, her hands dropping to her lap. She twisted the key again, but only got a stubborn *whop,* then silence.

''What's wrong?'' Lily asked.

''I don't know,'' she said, popping open the hood. ''I'll try to see.''

She got out, propped the hood up, and stared at the menacing mass of wires, hoses, and mystery objects underneath. Who was she kidding? She hardly knew what she was looking at. She chewed her thumbnail as she studied the battery, her leading suspect, because it was one of the few parts she could identify. Her brother, who had an interest in cars as a teenager, had talked of alternators, batteries, and generators. All those things and worse could cause a car not to start.

She sighed as a sick feeling spread over her. Poor Lily. She had been so excited about the fair. In frustration, she gave the radiator cap a resounding slap.

"Ouch," she muttered, massaging her palm with her other hand.

"Have you tried kicking it?"

Erin's heart thumped at the sound of a familiar baritone voice. She whirled to find Wyatt standing behind her, his hands resting on his hips.

Erin clamped her smarting hand against her chest. "Where did you come from?"

He smiled wryly. "I'm the man next door, remember?" The slanting autumn sunlight made the touches of silver in his dark hair glisten, and played over the cleanly sculpted lines of his face.

Erin turned back toward the open hood to avoid his sparkling indigo gaze. He was handsomer than she wanted to acknowledge. "Weren't we supposed to be keeping a civil distance?" she asked.

"That was the agreement. But I couldn't help but notice you were having car problems."

Erin turned back toward him. "You notice a lot for a man who doesn't believe in being a nosy neighbor."

"Wy-att," a little voice interrupted.

He stepped around to the passenger side. "Good afternoon, Lily." Erin detected a sudden tightness in his voice.

"We're going to the fair."

"Is that so?"

Wyatt, clad in jeans, a blue flannel shirt, and hiking boots, reappeared on the other side of the raised hood. "I'm here to help, but if you don't need me, I'll go back and mind my own business.''

Erin bit her bottom lip. ''It's nice of you to offer. I guess you can take a look,'' she said grudgingly.

Wyatt leaned over the engine for a moment. ''Well, all the parts seem to be here.''

Erin looked at him warily. ''They don't teach much about cars in law school, do they?''

He grinned crookedly. ''Actually, no. My mother taught me everything I know.''

''Your mother?''

''Her father owned a spark plug factory. My father eventually took it over.''

''I should have known.''

''Do you mind if I try to start it?'' he asked.

''You're welcome to try,'' she said with a shrug.

But the engine balked once more and Erin's heart sank.

Wyatt climbed out of the little car, his long legs barely clearing the door. ''This car probably won't be going anywhere today. My guess is that it needs a new battery. But I wouldn't rule out the alternator.''

Erin helped Lily out of the front seat. ''I'm so sorry, honey, but we're not going to be able to go.''

The child's eyes clouded and her chin fell. Erin, knowing that tears could come at any moment, knelt and pulled her close.

Wyatt closed the hood with a firm thump.

Erin stood. ''Thank you for trying to solve the problem.''

''Part of the problem is solved,'' he said, dusting off his hands. ''I'm taking you and Lily to the fair.''

Erin blinked. Lily fidgeted excitedly in her arms. ''But we can't let you go to all that trouble. You're busy and the fairground is fifteen miles away.''

"Nonsense," he said. "All you have to do is point the direction. And on Monday, you can call the garage. It's that simple."

"I don't know what to say," Erin responded.

"Say yes," he ordered, "or what I'm about to do will constitute abduction."

A twinkle appeared in his eyes as he grasped her shoulder firmly and led her toward his car. His touch made her blood sing through her veins. That was a clear warning to her. She needed to spend less time with this man, not more.

"We're going!" Lily squealed, skipping a few paces ahead. "We're going to the fair!"

"I'm still waiting for an answer," Wyatt said, his hand remaining casually on her shoulder.

She gave him a tight-lipped smile. "Our going to the fair seems to be a foregone conclusion."

He responded with a grin that hinted of victory and ushered them to his driveway where the BMW sat parked. She stood by as he unlocked the doors. She was only doing this for Lily, she told herself. And, no doubt, she conceded, so was he.

Silently, Wyatt helped the little girl into the backseat, snapping her seat belt into place. Then he opened the front door for Erin. She slipped inside, feeling the cool, smooth, unmistakable touch of leather underneath her. Wyatt, settling in behind the wheel, turned to her and playfully crossed his fingers before starting the engine. But his motor came to life instantly, purring like a kitten, unlike the unpredictable alley-cat growls of her own little car.

With one hand locked with a casual strength on the steering wheel, he turned to Erin. "I know the way to San Jose, I've been twenty-four hours from Tulsa and I once found

Lukenbach, Texas, but I don't know the way to the Maple County Fairground. Which way is it?''

''Drive to the village, then take Highway 13 east,'' Erin directed. ''I'll show you.''

Wyatt put the car in gear and backed out of the driveway.

''San Jose, Tulsa, and Lukenbach seem unlikely destinations for someone like you,'' Erin mused out loud.

He glanced at her with interest. ''What do you mean, *like me?*''

''You know,'' she said, eyeing the wood paneling on the dash.

''No, I don't. Tell me.''

''I would have associated you with more exotic destinations,'' she offered cautiously.

Wyatt halted at Maple Springs's sole traffic light. ''Like Borneo, Tasmania, Transylvania?''

''I know about Transvania,'' Lily interrupted from the backseat. ''That's where Dracula lives.''

Wyatt cocked an eyebrow in surprise.

''One of the older children in her car pool is going through a Dracula phase,'' Erin explained.

''I see,'' he said, turning onto the highway.

''London—that's you,'' she said.

''I've been there, too, in addition to having spent a rainy night in Georgia.''

Erin looked at him quizzically. ''That sounds like a song.''

His jaw was firm, but she caught a glint of mirth in his eyes as he glanced toward her. ''Very good. When I was in college, I decided to see the country one summer, letting songs be my guide. That's how I ended up in Lukenbach.''

''I see,'' Erin said. ''Was it 'London Bridge Is Falling Down' that sent you flying off to England?''

''It was a cruise,'' he answered; ''at least the first time. No, that came at a later time in my life,'' he said, his expression darkening.

Lily began to sing softly to herself. ''London Bridge is falling down, falling down, falling down, London Bridge is falling down, my fair ba-by.''

Erin caught Wyatt glancing at Lily in the rearview mirror. Although the corners of his mouth were tipped in a little smile, his eyes were clouded. Erin shifted uncomfortably. She wondered if Wyatt was thinking of his own child. As Lily switched to ''Do You Know the Muffin Man?'' Erin tried to relax and enjoy the rolling Vermont countryside with its centuries-old farmhouses and steepled churches.

Despite the pastoral views slipping past the windows, her awareness of the man beside her overpowered her senses. He smelled faintly of spice and freshly cut cedar and when he spoke, his rich, deep tones stirred something inside her. She found herself stealing glances at him, his clean profile, the shadow of his beard, his broad shoulders. An alarm bell sounded sharply in the deep recesses of her brain. How could she be having these reactions to a man who once tried to take Lily away from her, whose intentions could be questionable, still?

''Are we there yet?'' Lily asked, seemingly having grown tired of singing.

''Are we?'' Wyatt asked teasingly, glancing at Erin.

''Just about.''

''If I recall from my own childhood, 'just about' means a light year and a half,'' Wyatt said.

''As you've probably discovered, the older you get, the faster the clock runs,'' Erin said. ''We'll be there in two minutes, at the most.''

Just around the bend, the fairground appeared, its entrance marked with a bright yellow banner. Striped tents rippled under a clear blue sky. Whirling and rotating rides glinted in the sun.

"The Boston Pops it isn't, but next to the syrup and the foliage seasons, the fair is the year's biggest event in Maple County," Erin explained.

Wyatt, who showed no sign of being impressed, parked the car. Lily, in her excitement, scrambled out without assistance and dashed toward the rides.

"Wait," Erin called, reining her in by the backpack. "Let's hold hands."

Erin glanced up at Wyatt, who was watching them closely. She could hardly imagine his doing the things that fair-goers do—examining home-canned produce or looking at the prize-winning dairy cows. "I hope you won't be too bored," she said.

"Not at all." His tone was mildly formal. "You lead and I'll follow."

They walked through the buzzing crowds to the merry-go-round where Erin quickly purchased a ticket before Wyatt could offer to pay the fare. As the ride came to a halt, Erin led the child to the platform. Just as she reached down to lift her up, Wyatt took Lily from her arms, his hand brushing hers, sending prickles up her arm. She watched as he placed her on a white pony almost as effortlessly as if she'd been a feather. Erin, with Wyatt so close that she could almost feel the heat of his body, stood back and watched Lily bob up and down to a piped calliope version of "The Blue Danube Waltz."

"Are you thinking, as I'm thinking, how ironic it is that we're standing here together?" Wyatt asked after a moment of awkward silence.

"It couldn't get much more ironic," she said, purposely keeping her eye on the ride.

"You know, Erin, in the legal world, lawyers opposing each other in the courtroom can actually be friends privately."

Her gaze snapped to his. She didn't know what to say, only that the past was still too near and too raw. But she couldn't say that aloud to a man who was giving up an afternoon to take a child to the fair.

To her relief, the merry-go-round halted and Wyatt stepped away to pluck Lily off. Her face was flushed with excitement as she ran toward Erin.

"I get two more rides, don't I?" she asked breathlessly.

"Yes, sweetie."

"Only two?" Wyatt asked.

"We're on a bud-get," Lily explained.

Erin's stomach tightened. She looked at Wyatt for clues of disapproval, but there were none.

"I think I could scrounge up a dollar or two for an extra ride," he said. He bent toward Erin's ear and added softly, "You're wise not to overdo the rides. They can upset some children's stomachs."

Erin smiled with relief.

Amid the shouts of carnival barkers, they strolled through the midway, where Erin quite literally bumped into Tabitha Penobscot and her son, Caleb. Erin made all the proper introductions, noting, with a tinge of annoyance, that Tabitha was eyeing Wyatt with unabashed approval.

"Maybe Lily would like to see the baby animals in the show barn," Tabitha said to Erin.

Lily nodded brightly.

"One of the lambs is ours," she explained. "Caleb and I can take Lily. We won't be gone long."

Erin gave Tabitha a look of mild vexation. She knew what she was up to and, contrary to what Tabitha probably thought, she didn't want to be alone with Wyatt.

"We'll come along," Erin offered quickly.

"It's crowded enough over there with all those kids and strollers," the older woman said. "Jump on a ride or something. We'll meet you right here in about a half hour or so."

Chagrined, Erin watched as they disappeared into the crowd.

"Come on," Wyatt urged. "There's the Ferris wheel. You can give me an aerial tour of Maple County."

Before she could answer, he took her hand. "Hurry, they're boarding now."

She ran alongside him, oblivious to almost everything but the heat of his hand radiating through hers. Next, an attendant was securing a safety bar across their laps. The car lifted slowly into the air, gaining momentum on its way to the top. Below, the surrounding countryside began to spread out like a quilt.

"There's Maple County," Erin said, trying to ignore the tantalizing touch of his knee against hers.

The corner of his mouth quirked. "It wouldn't sprain your tongue to tell me more, would it?"

Erin averted her eyes from his, focusing on the shrinking tents below. "It's Vermont's leading producer of maple syrup and a popular destination for foliage tourists."

"I see. Thank you for that encyclopedic information."

Erin turned to find his eyes dancing with amusement. His gaze dropped to her lips. Her heart leaping, she quickly turned away. "You can contact the Chamber of Commerce if you want to know more, but even they are chatty only up to a point. If too many people knew the charms of Maple County, they would move here and spoil it. Enough eccentrics have moved in as it is.'' She turned back, concentrating her gaze on him with the precision of a laser.

Wyatt responded with a roguish smile.

''I'm glad you're enjoying yourself.'' Her voice was uneven.

''Thank you,'' he said smoothly. ''But rest easy. As beautiful as Maple County is, you don't have to worry about my becoming a permanent resident. By Christmas, I'll be back in Boston where I belong, amid the exhaust fumes and dying trees. I'm a Bostonian, true and blue.''

That was a point Erin wasn't going to dispute. Instead, she watched in silence as the ground faded away as their car made another ascent to the top. Suddenly, a grinding noise ripped through the air. The ride came to a jolting halt, sending her heart scurrying to her throat and nearly lifting her out of her seat. Wyatt threw a protective arm around her.

''What happened?'' she asked amid the cries and shouts of the other passengers.

''The noise sounded like the grinding of a gear,'' he said. ''Don't worry. They'll get us down. Have you ever heard of anyone growing old on a Ferris wheel?''

The heat of his strong fingers burned into her shoulder as she stared bleakly at the ground. ''Lily, Tabitha and Caleb—they won't know we're up here.''

Suddenly, an amplified male voice filled the air. ''Stay calm, folks. Just a little mechanical problem. We'll have you down within a half hour.''

Workers began erecting barricades around the base as toy-sized men carried what appeared to be toolboxes. But time dragged on as Erin anxiously searched the ground for

Lily and the Penobscots. Finally, she spotted them walking toward the growing crowd.

"There they are," she pointed with relief.

Wyatt slipped his arm away from Erin's shoulder. He took his billfold out of his back pocket and a quarter out of his front pocket.

"I don't think that tossing them a quarter will speed things up," Erin said dryly.

Wyatt chided her with his eyes. "You overestimate me."

He pulled a check from his billfold.

Erin looked at it, puzzled. "I don't think they take checks."

"Don't be silly," he said. "You must have a pen in that purse somewhere."

She produced one from her little string wallet. Wyatt took it and scrawled "void" on one side and began writing a note on the other.

"We're close to the top. We'll wave. Watch for us. We'll be down before you know it." He signed it "Aunt Erin and Wyatt."

Erin watched as he folded the note around the quarter and wrote "LILY" boldly on the outside. He leaned to the side of the car where Lily and the Penobscots stood and let it drop. A man from the crowd picked it up and, within moments, Erin saw him hand it to the little girl. The Penobscots gathered around her and, in a moment, her hand went up and they waved back.

"Feel better?" Wyatt asked. The wind blew his thick hair across his forehead, giving him a boyish look.

She nodded. "Thank you. A clever trick."

"I always try to keep a few up my sleeve."

Erin smiled, but, underneath, his words brought a flicker of concern.

Wyatt settled back against the seat, his shoulder touching hers and making her veins jump. His body was lean, yet powerful, his cheekbones burnished by the autumn sun. Erin guessed that any number of women in Maple County would gladly trade her place in the stranded car next to Wyatt Keegan, but for her, he posed entirely too much danger.

"If it were night, we could stargaze," he said, looking out over the hazy, blue sky. "If there were clouds, we could look for cloud pictures. I guess we'll just have to talk."

"I'm speechless," she said.

He turned toward her and put his hand on the back of the seat. His fingers were within touching distance of the nape of her neck. He crossed an ankle over the opposite knee and, propping an elbow on the side of the car, rested his head casually on his fist. "Tell me, is your life always this topsy-turvy?"

Erin eyed him suspiciously. "What do you mean?"

"Within a few weeks' time you've fallen off the roof, your car has gone kaput, and now you're stuck in the air, in a Ferris wheel."

Erin frowned. "Don't forget to add that my sweet, dear neighbors moved away and you moved in."

A smile teased the corners of his mouth as he cast her a sidelong glance. "Never a dull moment in the March household."

His sentence was punctuated by a clang, then a lurch, as the ride started moving again. Cheers rang up around them. Erin breathed a deep sigh of relief as their car moved toward the ground.

Barely had the attendant released them from the car when Lily was in Erin's arms. She lifted the child up and squeezed her tight. ''I thought you were never, ever, ever going to come down,'' Lily said.

She scrambled from Erin's arms to Wyatt's, throwing her arms around his neck.

''I'm glad everybody's all right,'' Tabitha said, giving Erin a hug. The old woman turned toward Wyatt. ''And that note—that's Yankee ingenuity.''

Wyatt grinned, but Erin was surprised once again to see that mysterious flicker of sadness in his eyes as he held Lily.

''Caleb and I need to get back to the store,'' she said. ''Enjoy our fair, Mr. Keegan.''

''What next?'' Wyatt asked as the Penobscots left.

''Two more rides and a candy apple,'' Lily reminded.

She took spins on a miniature fire truck and inside a Cinderella carriage. Wyatt treated her to a Gypsy fortune-teller who said that there would be snow in her future—a foregone conclusion in Vermont, Erin thought. Lily left the fairground, weary, happy, and sitting on Wyatt's shoulders, while Erin carried a half-eaten candy apple.

They drove home in near silence. Wyatt filled the lull with a CD of rippling classical music that seemed to give the Vermont countryside a little added magic. It was then that she realized that despite the fact that the Ferris wheel was on the fritz, she'd enjoyed herself. She'd even enjoyed some of the moments with Wyatt. Troubled by her attraction to him, she tried to convince herself that she didn't enjoy being with him, that it was just the thin air at the top of the Ferris wheel.

Wyatt parked the BMW in his driveway, got out, and opened Erin's door. He took Lily from the backseat, but she resisted being put down by clamping her legs around his waist. ''Do you have to go, Wyatt?'' she asked.

''I'm afraid so, Lily,'' he said, searching the child's eyes. ''We've had enough adventures for one day.''

''Would you take me home on your shoulders?''

''Lily,'' Erin cautioned, ''Wyatt's tired.''

Ignoring Erin, he hoisted the child onto his shoulders. She placed her hands under his chin and beamed as he strode up to their front porch. ''There's your little package,'' he said to Erin, setting Lily down in front of the door, ''delivered safely.''

''Wyatt, thank you.''

''You're welcome,'' he said, his voice suddenly taking on a tone of formality. He turned and started toward the steps.

''Wy-att,'' Lily called, ''I want to kiss you good-bye.''

Erin tensed.

Wyatt stopped at the edge of the front porch, hesitated for a split second, and turned. He knelt on one knee and took the child into his arms. When he did, Lily planted a wet kiss on his cheek.

He lifted her bangs with his thumb and kissed her gently on the forehead. His expression, once again, turned sad. Then he walked away in silence.

Chapter Five

Erin sat at her desk and frowned. There were a number of things bothering her and they fell into two categories: her bank balance and Wyatt Keegan. A new car battery, a tune-up and Lily's preschool tuition had done considerable damage to the former. The latter had given what little peace of mind she had left a good clobbering. She glanced out the window under its swag of Irish lace to find the sky a pewter gray. With another hard rain, the roof could spring another leak.

The store of pottery that her brother and sister-in-law had left behind would probably bring several thousand dollars, but that was their legacy to Lily, and Erin vowed never to sell it. Some pieces were displayed on the living-room mantel. One was a plate with a simple floral design. The other was a whimsical blue-glazed pot with a little twist of a handle on the lid. The rest was carefully packed away in boxes in the attic. They were now covered with plastic—just in case. The kiln in which they were fired remained in the shed in back, just as Stephen and Carrie had left it.

Erin chewed on a pencil already rough and splintered from her ruminations. It should be clear to Wyatt by now that she and Lily squeaked by from month to month. It wasn't the financially secure and orderly existence that he'd argued she should have. But they always made it and had everything they needed—everything, of course, but a new roof. And her aging little car? Well, she'd rather not think about that.

She didn't want to think about Wyatt Keegan either but he kept slipping into her mind, like ghosts are said to go through walls. Her mind flashed back to his unsettling gaze, his wry smile, his rare but rich laugh. She touched her shoulder where his hand had been and panicked. The man who had strode into the courtroom with an air of confidence that bordered on superiority had been so easy to dislike. But the man who carried a little girl on his shoulders wasn't.

Her thoughts were interrupted by the electronic chirping of the fax machine. She pulled out the paper and silently rejoiced. The antique Swedish trunk she'd initiated a search for had been located in a village near Oslo. A picture would follow for the buyer's approval. Erin loved the thrill of the find. Every day was like a treasure hunt. Today, she was searching for antique Portuguese tiles for a mansion bathroom in Rhode Island and a large quantity of old Russian samovars to decorate a restaurant in New York. But she was impatient for the business to grow and had to find ways to make it expand faster or she and Lily were eventually going to be dining under umbrellas.

Just as she reached for her rotating index card file, Lily scampered into the room, her face bright. A large sheet of art paper fluttered in her hands. "Look what I made, Aunt Erin."

The child laid it on Erin's desk with a flourish. It was a drawing of their bungalow, colored with bright, clear, crayon hues. The roof and the shutters were the proper dark green and the oversized Swedish mailbox was the proper red. Overhead, the waxy blue sky was punctuated with a big, yellow dot of a sun. But that wasn't all. Standing next to the house were four figures, a woman, a child, a dog, and a man. Erin's eyes narrowed as she studied the male figure.

"That's Wyatt," Lily explained, pointing a chubby finger at what almost appeared to be a halo of black hair.

"It certainly is," Erin said, injecting a lightness into her voice that she didn't feel.

"I'm going to give this to him for a present," the little girl announced.

Erin's heart gave a hard thump. "Lily, this is very nice," she finally managed to say, "but tell me something. This is our house and just you and I and Wiggles live here. Why did you put Wyatt in the picture?"

"Because I *like* him," she said without hesitation. "I wish he could do things with us forever and ever."

Erin took a deep breath and pulled her close. Her hair smelled faintly of baby shampoo. "Try not to get too attached to him. In a few months, he'll be moving back to Boston and we might not see him again."

A puzzled look crossed her small heart-shaped face. "But he's our friend."

Erin swallowed hard. "There are different kinds of friendships, Lily. Some of them last just for a little while and some last for a lifetime. Our friendship with Wyatt will probably be a short one because he is leaving. If we left Maple Springs, we couldn't be friends with Tabitha and Caleb in the same way. We couldn't see them as much or talk to them as much. Think of the Swayzes. We are still friends, but it's hard to be friends in the same way."

"But Mr. and Mrs. Swayze are going to come back and see us," she said.

"I'm sure they will."

"And Wyatt can come back and see us," she added innocently.

Erin hesitated for a moment. "Yes, I suppose he could, but he'll be very busy. The Swayzes are retired. They have much more time than Wyatt."

A look of disappointment crept over the child's face and Erin's heart sank. After all this time, Wyatt Keegan was still complicating their lives.

The Penobscot General Store had been a fixture in Maple Springs for over one hundred years. There, Erin could get almost anything from a half-gallon of milk to a sap bucket to a woolen blanket. But she went there for Tabitha Penobscot's crusty charm as much as anything.

Today, she bought a bag of groceries and some socks for Lily which Tabitha rang up on a vintage cash register. Tabitha, who could add up short columns of figures in her head if she had to, had no use for computerized anything. Heaven forbid. What if snow took out the power lines?

That done, Tabitha turned the register over to Caleb, and slid Erin's canvas shopping bag to the far end of the scarred, wooden counter. Lily, standing by Caleb, studied the assortment of cheap candies in the glass case under the counter.

"Tabitha, whatever possessed you to leave me alone with that man?" Erin whispered.

" 'That man' doesn't look nearly as awful as you described him. In fact . . ."

"Appearances are deceiving," Erin said, cutting her off in mid-sentence.

"They certainly are. Lily was smiling and the two of you looked like a couple of ants on their way to a picnic.

It looked like all was right with the world. It looked like a date.''

Erin gasped. ''Tabitha, how could you get such an idea?''

''I just told you.''

''Well, it wasn't a date. My car wouldn't start and he came out to see what was wrong. When he couldn't fix it, he was forced to offer to take us.''

''Forced?'' Tabitha asked, scratching her nimbus of white hair.

''Well, you know. I suppose he didn't want to seem like an ogre to Lily. There she was close to tears. She'd been looking forward to the fair all week. He couldn't just go back in the house and pick up where he left off—threatening people with lawsuits or whatever he does in there.''

''Well, that shows what I know,'' she said wryly, tapping her fingers on a yardstick nailed to the counter for measuring piece goods. ''No fool like an old fool. And I went and got you stranded on a Ferris wheel with him. I'm awful sorry, honey.'' Her eyes narrowed with a barely discernible twinkle. ''Too bad it wasn't me instead.''

''Oh, Tabitha, you're impossible.''

Lily appeared with a red lollipop, compliments of Caleb.

''I've got some good news for you, Miss Lily,'' Tabitha said, bending over the counter. ''My little grand-nieces are coming to stay a few days. How would you like to come out to the farm and visit them? We'll have a wiener roast and maybe even a little hay-ride. You can see the little lamb again who won the prize at the fair. You can even spend the night.''

Lily looked at Erin for approval, her eyes bright. ''Can I, Aunt Erin?''

Erin smiled. ''I don't see why not.''

* * *

For the next few days, Lily talked of little else. It was with some relief to Erin that she spent so much time chattering about Laurie, who was a year older, and Annie, a year younger, that there was scarcely a mention of Wyatt.

After the fair, he'd gone back to minding his own business, which was exactly what both of them were supposed to be doing. But in the evenings, Erin had developed a habit of glancing out the window to see if he was at home. Once, she was surprised by his silhouette in the window and moved quickly away from the lace curtain.

In the meantime, the drawing of the four of them lay on the dining-room table. She must wait for the opportunity to give it to him, she'd told Lily. Perhaps that way she'd better understand that he was a man who wanted to keep his distance.

The next afternoon, Erin drove Lily to the Penobscot farm. The journey took them past five miles of rolling hills and maple groves. When Erin left, Lily and the nieces, two lively redheads, were combing the yard for suitable sticks for the wiener roast.

Erin drove back to the village with a void in her heart the size of the Penobscots' barn. She already missed Lily's chatter, her incessant questions about anything and everything, her child's perspective on the world. Erin shook her head at the cows in the field. Silly her. She could certainly manage without the child for twenty-four hours.

It was past six when she got home. The setting sun rimmed the trees in gold and cast deep shadows across her imperfect lawn. The house had seen better days, she thought, surveying the authentic but fading shutters and the perky autumn wreath on the door, but it had . . . well, character and, like a moth-eaten blanket, it was still good to snuggle up in.

She planned a quick supper and to work late into the night. She parked the car in the garage, hardly unable to notice that Wyatt's car was in his driveway. She was halfway up the steps to her front porch when she spotted a package by the front door. She picked it up to see that it was addressed to Wyatt. A corner of her mouth crimped. It wasn't the first time that the delivery service, knowing she worked at home, had left packages with her for the neighbors.

She glanced at the saltbox. All was normal and orderly, as usual. She'd walk over, quickly hand the package to him, and leave, careful to disturb his normal and orderly life only a jot. She'd barely give him time to say "Thank you." She wouldn't have thought to ring the bell at all, except that, perhaps, the package might contain something valuable, something he would need right away. It would, after all, be the civil thing to do.

She walked briskly up his long, brick walkway and rang the bell. The door quickly snapped open. Wyatt, with his tie loosened, his crisp, white shirttail almost out, and his shirt halfway unbuttoned, arched an eyebrow in surprise.

"Good evening," Erin said a bit stiffly. "They left this package for you at my house."

Thanking her, he tucked it under one arm and began rebuttoning his shirt, obscuring Erin's view of the curls of dark hair at the V neck of his undershirt. "Sorry," he said. "I was just on my way upstairs to change when the doorbell rang."

"No need to apologize," she said, turning. "Good-bye."

She'd gotten several steps away when she was startled by the touch of his hand on her elbow.

"You could at least wait until I say 'good-bye' back to you."

She looked up into the mischievous lights in his eyes and her blood stirred. He dropped his hand from her arm. "That's better. Give my regards to Lily and Wiggles."

"Lily isn't home. She's spending the night with the Penobscot nieces, but I'll tell Wiggles that you asked about him."

The corner of his mouth tightened into a suggestion of a grin. "Please, do."

She turned and got only a few more steps away when he called her name. She turned to find him striding toward her. His green silk tie was flipped over one shoulder and errant strands of dark hair fell over his forehead.

"Would you join me for supper?" he asked.

Erin was suddenly struck mute.

"That's not a very enthusiastic response," he said, resting his hands casually on his hips. "Let me approach this from another angle," he said, gazing up pensively. "I have several cartons of Chinese carry-out that I just brought home. Nice, hot and fresh. No additives or preservatives. It comes complete with egg rolls, fried rice, and a bottle of unopened wine. I can't possibly eat it all myself and I was taught that it's a sin to waste food. My family is very devoted to that principle—my Uncle Arturo in particular. He weighs three hundred pounds and still eats like there's no tomorrow."

A small smile sneaked across Erin's lips.

"Does that mean yes?"

Erin perused the question for a moment. He was, after all, being very nice and it was hard to say no even though the logical side of her brain was saying "proceed with caution."

"Yes," she relented.

Minutes later, after allowing Wiggles a quick romp outdoors and running a brush quickly through her hair, she was back at Wyatt's front door. The tan corduroy walking shorts she'd been wearing would do and so would the oversized red sweatshirt. One didn't dress up for Chinese carry-out. And one didn't dress up for a man unless she wanted his attention.

He came to the door, wearing rumpled chinos and a dark blue denim shirt, apparently not terribly eager to impress her either. Uncharacteristically, for Mr. Impeccable, he'd even skipped one of the middle buttons. Possibly, it was even missing. He looked momentarily distracted, even puzzled, then greeted her with a smile.

"I think I'm the guest you were expecting," Erin said.

"Indeed you are," he said, stepping back from the door. "Since I've arrived in Maple Springs, most of my guests have been unexpected."

Erin cast him an apologetic look. "Once again, I'm sorry. We really should discuss that ruined disk."

Wyatt's chin crinkled stubbornly. "Nonsense. Let's let bygones be bygones."

Erin shook her head adamantly, strands of hair swinging around her face. "I can do data entry. I can help you replace what you lost."

"It's not quite that simple."

"Then I can do something else to help make up for the lost time. I can rake leaves. You'll have tons of them, you know."

He pulled her inside and closed the door. He placed a hand on her shoulder and an index finger on her lips as his eyes bored determinedly into hers. The heat of his finger sent her blood skipping through her veins. "An apology is quite enough. You owe me nothing. Lily owes me nothing. Wiggles owes me nothing.''

Erin, her senses returning, took his hand gently away from her face. For the hand of someone whose tools were books and writing instruments, it was surprisingly large and strong.

''All you owe me at this moment,'' he said, dropping his hand from her shoulder, ''is the pleasure of your company. There's nothing else to say.''

''Yes, there is,'' she said, touching the placket of his shirt with a clear-glossed nail. ''You have a button unbuttoned.''

A barely discernible grin sneaked across his lips. ''It fell off, it seems. Is there a tailor in Maple Springs?''

Erin winced in disapproval. ''Only some Boston blue blood would ask a question like that.''

''Suppose you tell me what's wrong with asking a practical question?''

''Taking a shirt with a missing button to a tailor is not what practical people do. For centuries, New Englanders have prided themselves on their practicality. True, self-respecting Yankees sew on their own buttons. Some have even made their own buttons—and thread, too, for that matter.''

''I see,'' Wyatt said tersely. ''I'll have to tell my grandmother that. Her family arrived before the American Revolution. I don't think Grandmother ever sewed a stitch in her life. Didn't need to. Maids and that sort of thing, you know.''

Erin frowned. ''You really don't know what I'm talking about, do you?''

He ran a hand through his abundant hair and feigned a

sheepish look. "I'll go out and buy a needle and a yard of thread tomorrow."

"Spool," she corrected. "It comes by the spool. But you needn't go out and buy anything. I'll loan you both and even show you how they work because Maple Springs has no tailor. And as for your Boston tailor, he's probably too busy letting out your Uncle Arturo's seams to sew on a button."

"I think a glass of wine would do you good," he said. "Come into the kitchen and I'll tell you more about my Uncle Arturo."

Erin, having been in Betty Swayze's kitchen countless times, knew the way. But it was apparent that it was no longer a woman's kitchen, with its objects of warmth and character—copper molds and plates on the wall and a crock of wooden spoons. It was a man's kitchen—spare and strictly utilitarian. The window was shorn of its checkered café curtains and the counter was almost bare except for food cartons and a bottle of French wine.

Wyatt took two wineglasses from a cabinet shelf and set them on the gray marble counter. He rolled his sleeves over muscular forearms, inserted a corkscrew in the bottle, and in one, deft, practiced motion, popped out the cork.

"I suppose if I were resourceful, like a true Yankee, I wouldn't need a corkscrew," he said teasingly. "I could just take out the cork with my teeth or perhaps break off the neck of the bottle on the edge of the counter. What do you think of that?"

Erin's nose twitched. "The word 'facetious' comes to mind."

"Sorry," he said, pouring each glass about half full. "I must be trying your patience."

She responded with silence.

"Oh, well," he said, handing her a glass. He held his own in mid-air and looked into her eyes. "To being good neighbors."

She touched her glass to his and a note of pure crystal rang out. Erin couldn't avoid the dark blue depths of his eyes nor ignore the odd little twinge under her heart. No matter what he did or said, he always seemed to have the most unsettling effect on her.

"Come on," he said, his expression now serious, "let's go sit down for a moment."

Wyatt led the way into the living room. He switched on two lamps, casting a golden glow across the room. Outside, the light had faded to a shade or two away from darkness. Erin sank into a beige Chippendale sofa that looked as if it could have been in the family since Chippendale. Wyatt, crossing one long leg over the other, sat across from her in an old wing chair slipcovered in a tiny blue and beige stripe. But the showpiece of the room was an antique Persian rug that was worn almost down to the weft.

"You said you were going to tell me about your Uncle Arturo," she said.

He looked at her over his wineglass. There was a touch of a smile on his lips. "I was wishing just a little that you might forget."

"I don't forget things."

"No, you don't," he said, the entendre clearly double. He stroked his chin thoughtfully. "Let me see. With Uncle Arturo, it's hard to tell where to begin. When he was younger, he was a philandering opera singer. He came by it—the singing part, that is—from his father, an Italian immigrant. He has a lust for two human pleasures, eating being one of them. The fact that he has seven ex-wives says something about the other."

Erin gulped.

"He thinks the rest of the family is hopelessly proper and humorless. He says someone needs to have some fun, so it might as well be him."

"I think I might like him," Erin said.

"I think you should stay away from him," Wyatt said quickly. "Beautiful blonds drive him mad."

A flush of heat crept up her cheeks at his assessment of her looks. "Well, then, I'll just stay here where it's safe—with you."

Wyatt set down his empty wineglass, leaned back in his chair, and steepled his long fingers. He studied her for a moment, as if she were an especially confusing abstract painting.

"I think I detected a bit of irony there."

"Maybe," Erin said. "I didn't have an Uncle Arturo, but I had a spinster aunt, Elizabeth, whose motto was 'The more I know man, the more I love my dog.' She did it in needlepoint."

He blinked. "That gives me an idea that I might rank alongside Wiggles."

Erin smiled mischievously.

"Erin, I sense you don't trust me. Is that true?"

She shifted uncomfortably. His eyes were penetrating, expectant. "I find you complex, hard to read, sometimes preoccupied, and if you want to know the truth, sometimes downright stuffy."

A dark brow lifted. "I was hoping for something a bit more flattering. Is that the best you can do?"

"Well, I guess you can be funny once in a while—a bone-dry type of funny—and you're not too bad-looking, now that I think about it."

Slowly, a smile appeared on his lips. "Thanks. I'm trying to get back to my usual charming, albeit a bit stuffy, self but it hasn't been easy since . . ." His smile faded so suddenly that Erin was momentarily startled.

"Since what?" Her tone was cautious.

"Since I lost my wife . . . and my child."

She felt an ache of sympathy. "I understand, although losing a brother, like I did, is a different kind of loss."

"Thank you, but you needn't say anything. It's over. It won't happen again. I won't allow anything like that to happen again. If you don't fall in love, you don't lose the person you love. It's that simple. Another marriage is out of the question for me." His jaw took on a stubborn set.

Her heart constricted at the determination in his voice. "I'm sure a lot of people feel that way at first," she offered.

"My feelings are as strong now as they were at the beginning." A pause followed. "Come on," he said, his tone brightening, "let's talk about you." His gaze settled on her half-bare legs.

Feeling exposed, Erin grabbed a pillow and slapped it over her knees.

He smiled, making her bristle. "Now, let's see if I can regain my train of thought. I see you as someone who's distrustful and bears grudges. But you're also an admirable person."

Her fingers tightened over the pillow. "Do you usually admire people who don't trust you?"

"Not usually."

"Then what makes me different?"

"Your devotion and determination when it comes to Lily."

"That will never change," she said with a note of warning.

His gaze was intense. "Of course not."

Wyatt got up and took a step toward her. "Come on," he said, taking her hand, "we've almost forgotten about supper."

They reheated the moo goo gai pan and Szechuan beef and sat at a small drop-leaf table in the dining room. The only illumination was from a small lamp on a sideboard. Like the others, the room was spare and the walls bare, as they would be for a man who had no intentions of settling in.

"Lily is somewhat taken with you," Erin admitted.

Wyatt, laying down his fork, looked mildly surprised.

"I'm not quite sure how to deal with it," she continued.

Wyatt, the lamplight dancing along the planes of his face, swallowed hard. "It's ironic, isn't it?"

"It's that, at least."

"She really doesn't know about my past role in her life, does she?"

Erin shook her head. "I don't want to confuse or frighten her."

"Good. I wouldn't want her to see me as the bogeyman."

Erin, running a finger around the rim of her wineglass, shrugged. "You've been very kind to her, all things considered. I appreciate that. But there's the possibility she could become attached to you. And when you leave, she could be hurt. She has already had so many losses in her life—her parents, the Swayzes."

A troubled look crept over his face. "I'm sorry, Erin. I'll be very careful."

"I know you will."

Suddenly, Erin became aware of the soft spatter of rain

against the windowpanes and a chill that had filled the room. She thought uneasily of her roof.

"I'm rather inept in the kitchen," Wyatt said. "But I do manage a good cup of cappuccino. Perfect for a rainy night."

She watched as he deftly juggled cups, spoons, and froth, and sprinkled a dash of cinnamon on top of the finished product.

"Where did you learn that?" she asked.

"Grandmother's maid," he said. "Unlike Grandmother, I know the way to the kitchen. But unfortunately, once I get there, I hardly know what to do."

"They have books for that sort of thing, you know," Erin said. "They're called cookbooks."

"I've heard of them," he said mildly, emptying onto a plate an envelope containing two fortune cookies.

"I think I can manage to loan you one."

"It would be nice," he said, loading the coffee and cookies onto an old silver tray. "I'm running out of restaurants. I've been saving Buster's Chili Bowl and Pool Hall as a last resort."

The growing chill was even more apparent in the living room. Wyatt set the tray on the coffee table and strode over to the thermostat and turned on the furnace. It started with an efficient hum.

"It's a good furnace," Erin said. "The Swayzes ran it practically at full throttle."

Wyatt sat in the wing chair. "The cappuccino will warm you up in the meantime."

Erin cupped her hands around the steaming mug and sipped slowly. A slight rumble of thunder sounded outside.

Wyatt lifted the plate of fortune cookies. "See what tomorrow will bring." In the sparsely furnished room, his clear baritone seemed to bounce off the walls, then wrap around her.

She set down her cup, snapped the cookie in two, and pulled out the small ribbon of paper. "Long live disco." Erin touched her forehead. "I don't think Confucius said this."

"I admire a woman who knows her philosophy," Wyatt said, opening his. It was blank except for a picture of a happy face.

Wyatt frowned. "I'm afraid the Wangs are becoming entirely too Americanized. I should have guessed from their New England Patriot jackets."

Erin grinned, almost forgetting the problems she'd left at home, until a loud clap of thunder rattled the windowpanes. The noise sent them both to the window. Raindrops danced under the streetlight. She thought of the roof and began to worry.

"I really should go, Wyatt," she said, turning toward him. "I need to call the Penobscots to check on Lily, Wiggles is afraid of the thunder, and . . ." She stopped short of telling him her furniture might be afloat. "It was nice of you to invite me over. It was a nice evening."

"Surprised?"

"Maybe."

"I'll get an umbrella and walk you home," he said, plucking one from the hall closet.

They dashed out into the night with Wyatt holding the umbrella in one hand. His other arm was around Erin's shoulder, holding her close under the umbrella's shelter and sending her heart racing. She ran to keep up with his long strides. His arm slipped around her waist and he almost lifted her off her feet as they bounded up the steps. Under the wide shelter of the porch, Wyatt snapped the umbrella closed just before a sudden gust of wind sent a shower of water over them. Their eyes met in mutual surprise and they broke out in simultaneous laughter.

Wyatt, his shoulders wet and his dark hair glistening with droplets of water, pulled a clean handkerchief from his pocket and touched it to the icy spray trickling down her face. She felt the heat of his fingers at the nape of her neck and her heart went still. He raised her chin slightly and their gazes locked in one burning moment. Then he lowered his head and touched his lips to hers.

Chapter Six

The touch of his lips against hers, tentative at first, left her stunned. Before she could grasp what was happening, he pulled her into his arms and kissed her with a fervor that made her heart hammer against his chest and her blood roar. The kiss was sure, expert, and dizzying. It was filled with a need that made her knees go weak.

She answered his longing with her own, reaching up and touching his shoulders, then feeling the crisp hair at the nape of his neck. And for an instant, the night, the rain, and the contentious past that had divided them ceased to exist. She yielded to the gentle strength of his embrace, the heat of his touch. It was a man's touch, long absent from her life.

Then a flicker of reality appeared at the rim of her consciousness. Her mind grappled, reason struggling over impulse and yearning. She pulled away from him, her hands pushing against the firm and broad expanse of his chest.

''Please go home,'' she said raspily. She was as shaken by her response as she was by his kiss. She flung open the screen door, her heart drumming wildly. Inside, Wiggles let out a yap.

Wyatt grabbed her by the elbow, turning her toward him. His eyes blazed with intensity. ''I'm sorry,'' he said softly.

Erin glared at him. "Good. So am I."

His lower lip twitched. "That's not the impression I got."

Her cheeks burning, Erin took a quick sidestep, grabbed his umbrella from the porch, and thrust it firmly into his hand. It dripped on his shoes.

He whacked it against the porch railing to shake off the excess water and gave her an unappreciative look. Wiggles barked again.

"Good night, Wyatt." She fled into the house and closed the door with a snap. The window in the front door rattled faintly. Wiggles's tail, raised in anticipation of a warm greeting, dropped.

Erin stood frozen, her back to the door, her lips still tingling from his kiss. After a moment, she slid to the floor, sitting Buddhalike, with ankles crossed. She took Wiggles into her arms and absently stroked his long, silky coat.

What had possessed him to kiss her? What had possessed her to enjoy it? She didn't trust him. She didn't trust herself, and nothing good could come of it.

The roof hadn't leaked after all and Lily was delivered safely home the next morning in Tabitha's Jeep. Erin's joy in both was numbed somewhat by the fact she'd hardly slept. Lily, rosy-cheeked from a night of camping in the crisp autumn air, gave her and Wiggles each a hug and a kiss. Then she asked, "Did you see Wyatt?"

Erin's heart thumped. "Yes," she said, taking the little girl's backpack.

"What was he doing?"

Erin bit her lower lip, pretending to barely remember. More than ever, she feared Lily would become attached to him. Now, she was afraid of her own feelings as well. "Oh, he was doing just the usual things, coming home from work, having supper, going to bed,'' she said with a shrug of feigned nonchalance.

''Did you give him my picture?'' she asked.

Erin swallowed hard. ''No, sweetie. It's your present. You should be the one to give it.'' She had secretly hoped the picture and its worrisome implication would be forgotten.

''Okay,'' she said, seemingly satisfied.

''You haven't told me about your camping trip,'' she said, gently changing the subject.

Her eyes brightened. ''I cooked a hot dog on a stick all by myself. It was a long stick—about a mile long. Tabitha watched me.''

Erin smiled. ''I'm sure she did.''

''And then it thundered and I wasn't even scared, but Annie was. She's only three.''

''I'm proud of you for being so brave,'' Erin said, smoothing down Lily's bangs. She already heard part of the story from Tabitha when she had called her the night before. When it had begun to rain, Caleb had set the girls' tent up on the front porch of the old farmhouse. She felt yet another surge of gratitude for the Penobscots. They'd always been there for support, friendship, and encouragement. She'd needed all of it, and then some, while juggling childrearing and a business that demanded even more attention than Lily. It hadn't been easy. She wanted Wyatt, least of all, to know how difficult it still was.

Saturday brought out half the block in a leaf-raking frenzy. There was Mrs. Stahl, who, at eighty, still mowed her own yard. It was barely nine o'clock and she already had three neat piles raked up. There was Mr. Wainwright, who would have avoided such work entirely if his wife hadn't stood on the porch with a stern watch over him, pointing here and pointing there.

Erin, sipping coffee from a mug, watched from the living-room window, then surveyed her own yard. It was lightly carpeted with leaves from her lone maple, and plate-sized sycamore leaves that had blown over from Wyatt's. In short, it was a mess—another problem that would have to wait. She'd been up since five-thirty, tying up loose business ends, trying to do as much work as possible while Lily slept.

After breakfast, Lily had gone outside to feed bread crumbs to the birds. Erin, realizing she'd been gone longer than she should have been, set down her coffee cup and started toward the back door. Outside, she found the little girl standing in her little red wagon and peering over the picket fence that separated their backyard from Wyatt's.

"Lily," Erin whispered loudly, "what are you doing?"

The child whirled around and jumped out of the wagon with Wiggles leaping out after her. "Nothing," she said guiltily.

Erin took her by the hand. "Let's go in the house."

Lily wore a pout as Erin sat her down at the kitchen table. "Pumpkin, you're not to bother Wyatt."

"I wasn't bothering him. He was reading a book. I wasn't doing anything but watching."

Erin took a deep breath. "Did he see you?"

Lily nodded, her eyes wide. "He said, 'Good morning,' and I said, 'Good morning' back and then he went in the house. I was waiting for him to come back out."

Erin frowned. "He works hard and doesn't have much time to himself," she explained gently. "He needs privacy. He can't have privacy when a little girl is peeping over his fence. And remember, we promised that we would leave him alone and he promised not to bother us.''

Lily responded with a grudging look.

Erin felt a little twist of pain under her heart. She would somehow deal with the fear and confusion in her own heart, but she didn't want Lily to fret. The less both of them saw of him the better.

She treated Lily to lunch at a quaint hamburger stand in the village, then they strolled through a nearby park. Lily, wearing a red felt hat with a rolled brim, and Wiggles, outfitted in a purple bandanna, were pulled along in the wagon. Holding a yellow helium-filled balloon they'd bought along the way, she sang happily off-key. The air was sweet with the scent of fallen leaves and for a little while Erin forgot her troubles.

They came back in a flash as they neared home. Standing in front of his house, busily attacking leaves with a rake, was Wyatt. He glanced up at the approaching sound of the wagon wheels and his eyes locked with Erin's.

He rested his hands on the rake handle and surveyed Erin and her cargo. ''Hello,'' he said with an undertone of caution.

Erin's heart rattled inside her chest. ''Hello,'' she said benignly, as if speaking to a stranger. The exercise and cool air had imparted a glow of masculine vigor to his face.

He leaned over and touched Lily on the cheek. ''And hello again to you.''

Lily smiled sheepishly at him. ''Aunt Erin says I'm not supposed to peep in on you anymore.''

''Well,'' he said, shifting his gaze to Erin, ''I know from experience that Aunt Erin means what she says.''

Erin looked at him through narrowed eyes. ''I think we

should be going,'' she said, giving the wagon a tug. ''Good-bye, Wyatt.''

She'd only taken a few steps away when she detected the acrid smell of something burning. She stopped. No one burned leaves in Maple Springs. It wasn't permitted. She quickly scanned her surroundings, seeing nothing but Mrs. Stahl fussing over her chrysanthemums. It was when she turned to go home that she discovered a thin stream of smoke coming from Wyatt's kitchen window. She quickly pulled the wagon over to Mrs. Stahl's, asking her to watch Lily, then dashed off toward Wyatt.

''Something's burning in your kitchen!'' she yelled.

Wyatt dropped the rake as if it were on fire. ''Darn, the pot roast,'' he said, breaking into a run. Erin sprinted after him, rushing through the house into the kitchen. On the stove, a piece of cast-iron French cookware sat smoldering, smoke boiling ominously from under the lid. Before Erin could stop him, he grabbed one of the handles bare-handed and pulled it off the burner.

''Ouch!'' he boomed. His hand flew to his mouth and he bit down on it in a futile attempt to blunt the pain.

Erin's stomach lurched. She flipped off the heating element and grabbed his wrist at the same time.

''Let me see,'' she said, opening his hand to reveal reddened fingers. ''Oh, poor baby,'' she said, leading him toward the sink. Suddenly, she realized what had come from her lips and her cheeks turned to flame.

He flashed a crooked smile. ''I feel better already.''

''I'm used to talking to Lily,'' she said indignantly.

Seeing that his coy smile remained, she gave his arm a final yank toward the sink. She turned on the cold-water tap and thrust his hand under it.

He took a deep breath and blew out slowly. "By the way, where is Lily?"

"Don't worry. Your computer disks are safe. Mrs. Stahl is watching her."

"I was concerned about her well-being, not my disks," he said.

Erin gave him a dubious look. "Stay right here," she said. "I'll be right back. I'll bring you something else that will help."

"Don't worry about me," he said.

"Do you want your hand to stop hurting?" she asked pointedly.

"It might be nice," he said with a shrug.

Erin, her heart strumming, raced home and snapped an aloe vera leaf off a plant in the kitchen. She took a brief detour across the street to tell Mrs. Stahl and Lily what had happened.

"Did he cry?" Lily asked.

"Not in my presence," Erin said dryly.

Wyatt, his hand wrapped in a wet towel, was waiting for her in his doorway. He looked skeptically at the spike of green vegetation in her hand. "I'm afraid to ask where you went to medical school."

"It's aloe," Erin explained, slightly peeved. "It's a proven remedy."

Stepping inside, she took his hand, unwrapped the towel, and gently touched the cut end of the plant to his burned fingers. His eyes were not on what she was doing, but on her. She pulled back, her blood pulsing through her veins.

"Interesting," he said, inspecting his hand. "I suppose there's no cure for the pot roast."

Erin went to the kitchen and lifted the lid off the pot. Inside was an object that looked like a large lump of coal.

"You really meant it when you said you didn't know how to cook."

"I happen to like my meat well done," he said defensively.

Erin gave him a doubtful look.

"The truth is," he said, leaning against the cabinet with one foot crossed over the other, "I've been very preoccupied with something for the past few days."

Erin's gaze snapped to his.

"You know," he said, "we've got some unfinished business. If you promise not to dive through your front door after one of our visits as if the devil himself had come after you, I'd like to try once again to come to some sort of peace."

Erin looked at his hand and felt a pang of guilt. There were so many conflicting emotions rocketing through her that she didn't know what to say.

He breathed deeply, his solidly square shoulders rising, then falling. "Life can be complicated and painful. You and I especially should understand that. Let's not make it any more so."

She stared at him. He was extending an olive branch—with an injured hand, no less. How could she refuse it?

"Associating with Lily and me has gotten you a fall down the stairs, a punch in the gut, and a burn on the hand."

"Don't forget being stranded on a Ferris wheel," he added.

"Are you sure you want to proceed with this?" she asked.

There was a beat of silence. "Oh, why not?" he asked, shrugging one shoulder. "Suggest somewhere we can go—away from the hazards of Maple Springs."

She offered a tight but conciliatory smile and paused for a moment of consideration. "Well, there's always the foliage. The closest you've gotten to the forest lately is probably the paper your law books are made of."

Wyatt nodded thoughtfully.

"But I can't promise it will be hazard-free. Things happen, you know. That's life."

He gave her an off-center smile. "Don't worry. I'll take the risk."

The morning on which they were to leave was shrouded with mist. Erin just finished getting Lily ready for preschool when a horn beeped outside.

"There's your ride," she said, giving the little girl a kiss on the crown. She walked outside with her.

Idling in the driveway was a gleaming black Alfa Romeo convertible. Behind the wheel was a heavyset, middle-aged woman wearing a Dolly Parton wig and a pointed witch's hat. One child was strapped into the back and another into the front.

"Erin, dahling," she called, getting out in a swirl of black cloth. "Lily, how are you this morning, precious?" Without waiting for an answer, she gave the horn a few more light taps. "Jessie's here with a car full of cheer!"

The commotion brought Wyatt out of his house. He approached the fence with long, purposeful strides and gave Jessie a wary appraisal.

Erin made a quick introduction and watched as he politely shook Jessie's plump, manicured hand. But the crease of concern in his brow scarcely faded.

Jessie helped Lily into a backseat. Almost before Erin could say good-bye, Jessie was halfway out of the driveway, her pointed hat strapped under her chin, and rock music blaring from the dash.

Wyatt frowned. ‘‘You sent Lily off with that . . . that?’’

Erin bit her lip to keep from smiling. ‘‘That was Lily’s favorite car-pool driver.’’

The color in his face deepened. ‘‘But the woman’s nuts.’’

‘‘She’s the grandmother of the little boy who was in the front seat. She worked on Broadway for years. She’s always putting on a show.’’

He responded with a humorless look. ‘‘She’d better watch where she’s going while she’s doing it. Lily might not be safe in the clutches of a clown like that.’’

Erin’s mouth opened in surprise. ‘‘Listen to you. After your first encounter with Lily, you probably would have begged Jessie Whitlock to take her away as fast as that little sports car can go. Now you’re sounding like a . . . an overprotective father.’’

Wyatt stared at her, his face turning pale. ‘‘I wouldn’t want to see any child come to harm.’’

The emotion in his voice surprised her. ‘‘You can trust Jessie,’’ she said reassuringly. ‘‘That car might be a fast one, but she drives it like a Model-T.’’

Unconvinced, he responded with silence.

When they set out for the mountains, the morning sun had vaporized most of the mist and the foliage appeared through the windshield like splashes of color through a kaleidoscope. Wyatt handled the BMW easily through the twists and turns of the mountain highway but they’d only made senseless small talk for the first few miles of the journey. Erin wondered what he really thought of the way she was raising Lily and what messages he might be relaying back to the Holbrookes. She couldn't bear the thought of any more trouble from them.

He reached across the seat and brushed a finger across her cheek, lightly touching the corner of her mouth. "You're frowning. I hope you're not contemplating my latest offense, whatever that might be. We're here to make peace, remember?"

Her face tingled where he'd touched her. "I was just thinking," she said vaguely.

"I've been thinking about why I kissed you," he said, not taking his eyes off the road. The morning sun cast a rim of golden light around his nearly perfect profile. "I suppose I owe you some sort of explanation. I did it because I wanted to, just like a bee wants to go to a flower, because it's beautiful, it's sweet, and it fills a need."

She was too choked to respond. She avoided his eyes.

"Tell me why you kissed me back." His eyes met hers with a searing gaze.

"Because . . . it has been a long time," she said, fumbling for the right words. But they weren't all the words she could have used. She held back saying that she was drawn to him by a magnetism that was so powerful that it frightened her. It went beyond his dark good looks and seemed to transcend reason.

"A *long* time?" he asked. "What about the list of male visitors Lily rattled off?"

Erin shot him a menacing glance. "One is the plumber, who is so big he can barely get under the kitchen sink; one is the mailman, who has a wife and five children; and the other is Caleb Penobscot, a confirmed bachelor who would never leave his mother. Sorry to disappoint you."

The corner of his mouth crooked slightly. "Surely it hasn't been that long."

Erin briefly told him about her broken engagement. ''You see, it's different with a child. If a man couldn't love Lily as much as me, he might as well not love me at all. That's the way it has to be.''

His expression grew serious. ''I understand.''

An awkward lapse of silence followed.

''Does it bother you that Lily doesn't have a father, so to speak?'' he ventured.

''Lily has a father,'' she answered quickly. ''I keep him alive in her memory every day. She has his artwork, his kiln, and the poem he wrote for her on the day she was born. She has the sketches he made of her as she slept. I tell her everything about him that I can remember.''

Wyatt stopped the car at an observation point. He got out, opened her door, and gently took her by the hand. She lowered her head so he wouldn't see the tears stinging her eyes.

''Beautiful, isn't it?'' she asked as they looked down into a valley. The leaves glowed like jewels in the sun. The white steeple of an old wooden church rose from among the trees.

''Very,'' Wyatt said, turning toward her. His brow creased. ''You're crying.''

''I'm sorry. It's just . . .''

''I'm the one who should be sorry,'' he said, pulling her gently against him. She laid her cheek against the warm, hard muscles of his chest as his fingers slipped under her hair and stroked the nape of her neck. She could feel his heart beating under the soft flannel of his shirt. Her own was skipping wildly under her ribs. For an instant she lost all reason and took comfort in his strong, encircling arms. Then suddenly, he nudged her away. ''I'm sorry,'' he said. ''I'd better not get myself into trouble again.''

Erin managed a little smile despite the lump in her throat. "You'd better not."

They returned to the car and continued slowly along the curving road. Wyatt played soft classical music on the radio, as if to bridge the chasm of silence that had fallen between them. But Erin's senses were so attuned to the strong but worrisome magnetism of his presence that she scarcely heard the rippling notes.

Suddenly, he turned the music off and glanced at her. His expression was somber. "You should know something about Lily's case," he said.

Her gaze snapped to his.

He bit his lower lip as if steeling himself for what he was about to say. "Those of us who practice civil law don't usually take cases we don't believe in. The Holbrookes had a strong one."

The brilliance of the foliage suddenly dimmed. Erin shifted uneasily on the sleek leather seat. She wasn't sure she wanted to hear any more.

"The argument for two parents versus one is a strong one, especially when the orphaned child in question is barely two years old. Then there were the other factors—the Holbrookes' stability and financial means."

"Wyatt, I know what you're trying to say," she said, her voice unsteady.

He shook his head vehemently. "I'm not sure you do, Erin. Please, listen to me."

Erin turned away and squeezed her eyes shut as if to brace herself.

"Some of my beliefs came from personal experience," he said.

She slowly opened her eyes and looked at him. His chin had a troubled crinkle in it. "My mother abandoned the family when I was six, leaving my father and a few servants to raise my sister and me. Mother had money of her own and just went romping off to Paris. Being tied to boring Boston and its tedious family and social responsibilities hardly represented any kind of a life. At least that's the way she saw it.''

Her heart thumped in sympathy and surprise.

Wyatt stopped at a hilltop fruit and souvenir stand and turned toward her. The memory had dulled his eyes. ''She was quite the bohemian, flitting from one art circle to another, experiencing Paris like a teenager gone wild. There were letters at first, gifts on Christmas and on our birthdays, then they quit coming. Despite having help, it was difficult for my father. He had a factory to run and not a lot of time for us. My sister and I tried to compensate by convincing ourselves that we didn't need a mother—at least not one like ours—but the void was still there.''

Erin swallowed hard. ''I'm sorry.''

Wyatt shrugged. ''It's over. My mother died a few years ago without ever coming back. Happily, my father remarried a number of years ago, to a very nice woman.''

''I'm glad,'' she said.

''Lily is going to sense more and more that something is missing,'' he said cautiously.

His words seized her heart like a fist. ''No one abandoned Lily and no one ever will,'' she said firmly. ''As for not having another parent, I can't help the way things are. All I can do is my very best. I can't give her a lot of things, but she gets what she needs most—love, guidance, and attention, all in abundance,'' she said with a piercing stare.

Wyatt blinked, but said nothing.

Then Erin realized that she'd confirmed what he had no doubt suspected—that she and Lily were hardly living lives of luxury. ‘‘I do provide for her,’’ she added with an undercurrent of defensiveness. ‘‘Lily has everything she needs. And I have everything I need.’’

He touched a crooked index finger to his lower lip and studied her from under a shock of hair that had fallen across his forehead. A friendly glimmer appeared in his eyes. ‘‘Everything but a new roof?’’

‘‘Good Yankees are frugal,’’ she tossed back.

His gaze dropped to her lips. ‘‘Frugal indeed.’’

Erin's eyes narrowed in a mock warning. ‘‘Can't you just enjoy the scenery?

‘‘I am,’’ he said, his eyes flicking over her.

Erin shot him a look of impatience. ‘‘And you wonder how I can manage without a man,’’ she said, shaking her head.

‘‘Sorry. A man can't help being a true member of his sex.’’ He glanced over his shoulder at the fruit stand. ‘‘Come on. I'll buy you something to drink. I'll show you that a man is good for something.’’

They drank cups of hot apple cider, and Wyatt bought for Lily a small box of leaf-shaped maple candies. To that he added two jugs of apple cider for each of them to take home. ‘‘A peace offering,’’ he said wryly.

Erin's gave him a tight-lipped smile. ‘‘Thanks. I at least owe you a cooking lesson. In the interest of fire safety, of course.’’

As they drove back toward the village, the sun suddenly seemed to drop out of the sky and the wind kicked up. The tops of the trees swayed back and forth as if heralding an impending storm. ‘‘You may be seeing the last of the foliage,’’ she said. ‘‘The onset of winter here can take you by surprise.’’

‘‘So I've heard,’’ he said, maneuvering the car around a

hairpin curve. ''In the city, we lose touch with nature. One day, I suddenly couldn't remember if it was summer, winter, spring, or fall. I found myself looking out my office window for some sort of marker—a tree or a flower. I was that lost,'' he said, his tone suddenly solemn. He paused for a moment. ''Now I'm in Vermont and those things are in much sharper focus. I can look out the window and actually see things. But imagine my surprise when I found myself next door to you.''

''Imagine mine,'' she responded flatly.

Wyatt drove in silence, his brow furrowed as if he were still back in that stifling, urban world. A puzzled feeling came over her. What did he mean about being ''lost''? Just what in Maple Springs was he expecting to find?

Her anxiety deepened. Why had he asked her so many questions—questions reminiscent of those days in the courtroom two years before? She stole a glance at him and a jumble of conflicting emotions ricocheted within her. She was undeniably attracted to him, yet she was so afraid of him and the power he could wield.

''We're home,'' Wyatt announced, pulling into his driveway. He set the brake and turned off the engine. ''And guess what?'' he asked, turning toward her. ''Nothing happened. You're not the jinx you thought you were.''

''No, nothing happened,'' Erin said. But it seemed very much like something had.

Chapter Seven

Lily, outfitted in a secondhand teddy-bear costume, stood with her back to Erin. It was Halloween evening and moments before they were to go trick-or-treating, the tail had elected to fall off.

"Be very still," Erin ordered. She sat on the living-room floor holding the tail to the costume with one hand and a safety pin in the other.

"Aunt Erin, I love Wyatt."

The pin rammed through the folds of cloth and into Erin's finger. With a gasp, she jerked it back in pain, watching as a bead of blood formed on her fingertip.

Lily whirled around, her eyes wide. "You sticked yourself."

Erin quickly blotted the dot of red on the leg of her faded jeans. She wished Lily would get Wyatt off her mind. But how could she expect her to when she couldn't do it herself? Wyatt was interesting and amusing and handsome and could make a little girl laugh. He could make a big girl's blood jump in her veins.

"Lily," she said, taking her by the shoulders and turning her to face her, "that's very sweet. But don't forget that he's just here for a short time. Before we know it, he'll be gone."

"But can't he stay?"

Something inside her shriveled as she looked into her round, probing eyes. "No, Lily, he can't," she said firmly. "Please try to understand that."

The child's nose, on which Erin had painted a teddy-bearlike black triangle, twitched. Erin felt a chill. The sooner he was out of their lives, the better off they'd be. In the meantime, the best thing they could do was to stay out of his way.

That was easier said than done. They were barely out the front door when Lily, with her teddy-bear tail finally pinned on, although a bit off-center, gave Erin's arm a tug toward the saltbox. But it was soon evident that no one was home. Erin sighed with relief.

Lily's shoulders sagged. "But he'll come home later, won't he?"

"I don't know," Erin said, pulling her in the opposite direction. "I don't think he's expecting trick-or-treaters. If he were, he would be at home."

Lily's step lost its spring.

Erin felt a twinge of anger, anger at Wyatt for confusing Lily and for keeping her own emotions in a state of flux. For a man who resisted emotional involvement, his signals were hopelessly mixed.

They stopped first at Mrs. Stahl's. The old lady dropped a homemade popcorn ball, wrapped in wax paper and tied with black-and-orange ribbon, into Lily's bag and they chatted for a few minutes. Winter was coming early this year, she predicted. Yes, the squirrels were about their business early, just as they had been before the winter of '42. That was the year the snow came up to the windowsills.

At the Wainwrights', Mrs. Wainwright gave out the orders from an armchair while Mr. Wainwright gave out the toys. Lily got a ball and jacks.

They were on their way to the Heffners' down the street when car headlights appeared at the end of the block. Erin tensed as she recognized the BMW. It slowed and came to a stop on the opposite side of the street.

"Wyatt!" Lily called, breaking away from Erin and running toward the opening car door.

Erin, alarmed at how quickly she'd gotten away from her, dashed after her. "Careful, Lily," Erin scolded. "You didn't stop and look both ways."

Wyatt got out of the car and took the child by the hand. His eyes met Erin's and her pulse jumped. "Who do we have here, Goldilocks and one of the three bears?"

"I'm the bear," Lily announced.

"Who do we have there?" Erin asked dryly.

Wyatt smiled his crooked smile and placed both hands on Lily's shoulders. The sleeves of his white shirt were rolled up, the collar was unbuttoned, and his tie loosened, as if he'd just left the office. "I'm your escort service. You and Lily shouldn't be out by yourselves after dark."

Erin gave him a miffed stare. "Thank you, but no thank you. This is Maple Springs, where all the neighbors know each other, not the sinister back streets of Boston."

Ignoring her, he locked the car door, and took Lily's hand. The little girl was clearly enthralled. Erin was not.

"Well," he said, giving Erin a sidelong glance, "are you coming with us?"

Erin sighed and fell into step alongside them.

"Bears need honey," he told Lily. "Let's go find some."

They managed to finagle a small jar from Mrs. Swenson, the piano teacher. For added measure, she played a few bars of "The Flight of the Bumble Bee." At the Mc-

Coskeys', Lily got four chocolate Kisses, one for each year of her age.

Erin was silent as they strolled toward a small park. A child was giving one of the swings a workout, his ghost costume fluttering behind him.

''A penny for your thoughts,'' he said.

''Not a wise investment,'' she said. He was still holding Lily's hand and she wished that he weren't. It would just make things worse.

He looked at her skeptically, then turned to Lily. ''How about taking a few minutes to play in the park and sample some candy?''

She nodded eagerly. ''I can swing high. I'll show you.'' She thrust the bag of treats at him and ran off toward the playground equipment.

Wyatt sat on the edge of a picnic table and took Erin's hand. He gave her a tug toward him but she pulled away.

He raised a questioning eyebrow. ''I think you'd better tell me what's wrong.''

''I'm not sure it was a good idea for you to come along tonight,'' she said. ''We agreed that you would try to discourage Lily from becoming attached to you.''

His mouth tightened into a straight line. ''What kind of man would I be if I let both of you go tromping off into the night by yourselves?''

''We can take care of ourselves,'' she insisted.

He grabbed her hand and this time held it so tightly she couldn't pull away. ''Erin, I know what's out there,'' he said, his eyes glistening with intensity. ''Things can happen when you least expect them.''

''Look!'' Lily interrupted. ''Look at me!''

Erin's attention snapped across the playground where she was swinging mightily. ''Very good, Lily,'' she called.

Wyatt gave the little girl a thumbs-up, then released Erin's hand.

"I'm not naive, Wyatt," she said, massaging her wrist. It burned from the heat of his touch.

He sighed. "No, of course not. But a place like Maple Springs practically begs you to let your guard down. It's a postcard village with white picket fences and little old ladies who put up blueberry jam."

She stared at him, her blood stirring uneasily. "Nothing will happen to Lily under my watch."

Wyatt studied her for a moment, his expression darkening. "Nothing probably will. But things can happen despite your best intentions."

She turned away from him, feeling a swirl of mixed emotions. She wanted him to believe in her capabilities but how could he when his own life had been marked by loss?

"Can we go to some more houses, please?" Lily asked, scampering toward them.

"Just a few," Erin said. "It's getting close to your bedtime."

The child skipped ahead, her bag of loot swinging and the bear ears flopping.

"Halloween wasn't much at my house," Wyatt said. "One year, when I was about Lily's age, Grandmother sent the butler out to forage for some goodies for us. Indignant, he resigned the next day."

Erin couldn't help but smile.

Wyatt returned the smile broadly. "Do something for me."

"What's that?" she asked.

"Smile more often."

"Tell me another story."

"You tell *me* one."

"My brother and I played a two-headed monster in a Halloween skit. We wore one costume and had to appear as if we had only two arms and two legs. We practiced and practiced until we got it right. But just as we went onstage, the class bully dropped the class gerbil down the neck of the costume and we tore across the stage going in two directions at once. As the Maple Springs *Clarion* said, 'A good time was had by all except for the March children and a gerbil named Fred.' "

Wyatt laughed richly.

"I didn't know you could laugh," Erin said.

He gave her shoulder a quick, brotherly squeeze. "Thanks for helping me get back in the habit."

They turned the corner to the next block where one of Lily's preschool classmates lived.

"You and your brother were close?" he asked.

Erin nodded, her nerves still dancing from his touch. "We both had artistic leanings. We spent a lot of time together drawing. His interests evolved into pottery and mine into interior design. Art is something I try to encourage in Lily. It's a good form of self-expression for her." She thought fleetingly of the familylike portrait she'd done of them and Wyatt, and her heart stirred uneasily.

At the end of the block, Lily's bag began to drag and she began to straggle.

"This is quite a haul, Pumpkin," Erin said, taking the sack from her. "Let's go home."

The little girl offered no protest, only a yawn. Suddenly, Wyatt bent down and picked her up with such grace of movement, it was as if she were weightless. Lily fit easily into the crook of his arm and lay against his shoulder. Her hood had slipped off and her dark hair fanned across the white cloth of his shirt. Erin's heart thumped at the sight of them. It seemed so natural, yet she knew that before her was a scene that shouldn't be.

They walked home in silence except for the sounds of their own feet on the sidewalk. What had begun as an Indian summer evening was turning into a night with a frosty edge. Lily's head bobbed contentedly on Wyatt's shoulder.

"She's asleep," he whispered as they stood on Erin's front porch next to a large, lopsided jack-o'-lantern. "I can carry her inside if you like."

Erin shook her head. "Thank you, but that won't be necessary."

"I know," he filled in quickly, his gaze intense, "you can take care of yourselves."

Offering no response, she set Lily's bag of treats on the porch and unlocked the door.

Lily's head lifted from Wyatt's shoulder.

"You're home, little one. Let's put you down now," he said, bending and letting her slip from his arms.

As Erin reached for the child, her hand brushed Wyatt's rough cheek. She took a quick breath. "Let's say good night to Wyatt," Erin said finally.

He knelt and she placed her arms around his neck. " 'Night, Wyatt. You can have some of my candy."

"Thanks, but I'm sweet enough."

Lily smiled.

He rose, his eyes meeting Erin's. "I know you don't need me or anyone else, but I'll be in the wings. No gerbils, I promise."

Her fingers tightened on Lily's shoulders. "Good night, Wyatt."

She stood on the front porch and watched as his tall form disappeared into the night. No, she didn't need him to help her take care of Lily or to meet the challenges of life. But suddenly she was confronted with the alarming realization that she needed him in a more elemental way. She needed his touch. She needed to hear the sound of his voice, and that just wouldn't do at all.

The next week was a blessing. A flurry of orders came in that left Erin too busy to think about much else but getting them filled. Scores of boxes of wooden Christmas decorations arrived from Germany. The antique Portuguese tiles had been shipped, except there was an error and they were sending three hundred too many. And the Polish pottery had finally found its way to the port in Boston and Mr. Didier had agreed with a haughty sniff to take half of it. The other half would go to specialty shops throughout New England. Then came Quimper pottery from France and an antique bar from an English pub.

That meant a sudden swell of money into Dream House Imports. That also meant the roof was going to get fixed before winter.

A telephone call from the Swayzes had excited Lily, along with fruit and a T-shirt they'd sent from Florida. A preschool field trip to a wood-carving workshop and a classmate's freshly broken arm had given her something to talk about for hours, distracting her from the goings-on at the house next door.

But Erin wasn't so easily distracted. As the pop-pop-pop of the roofers' nail guns filled the air, she thought of their work as symbolic. It was added proof she could manage her affairs perfectly well. Amid all that din, Wyatt had to notice.

The new roof was barely on before the air inside the house began to chill and the wind began to whistle through the trees. Erin, who had been chatting with a supplier of Irish linen, hung up and went to the window. Outside, flakes of snow as big as cornflakes spiraled through the air in a slow descent to the ground. Erin watched in surprise. They were falling so thickly that Mrs. Stahl's house across the street was reduced to little more than an outline.

Just as her mind jumped to the thought of Lily at school, the phone rang. It was one of the car pool mothers. A major storm was brewing. This afternoon, she was picking up the children early.

Nervously, Erin went back to the window. November snowstorms were rare in Vermont, so unusual that the only one she could remember was when she was a child. The snow usually arrived just in time for Christmas. But it was here today, nevertheless. She braced herself with a cup of cocoa and went back to work.

Lily arrived about twenty minutes later, breathless, bright-eyed and red-cheeked. Could they take out the sled? Could they make a snowman?

"Yes, but first things first," Erin said, taking off the child's coat and making sure her snowy sneakers were left by the door. "Sit down and I'll get you some cocoa."

Lily sat at the dining-room table and Wiggles jumped into the chair beside her. In the kitchen, Erin could see that the backyard was already blanketed in white.

"Aunt Erin," Lily called, "I'm cold."

Erin took the mug of cocoa out of the microwave, balanced a plate of vanilla wafers on top, and, on the way to the table, jiggled the ancient thermostat on the dining-room wall.

Lily was halfway through her second cookie when a metallic groan rose up through the heating registers. It was followed by a rattle, then a clang so loud that it moved Erin off her seat.

"What was that?" Lily asked, wide-eyed. Wiggles had jumped into her lap.

"It sounded like the furnace. Let me go see."

Erin ran down to the basement where the hulking maze of pipes and vents sat. And at that moment, it sat as still as death itself. In its belly, where a fire usually danced, there was nothing but darkness.

"Oh, darn," she said, giving it a kick in frustration. The noise reverberated through the basement and back up through the pipes.

The furnace man, a relative of Mrs. Stahl, said he'd get there as soon as he could, whenever that might be. In the meantime, she took the sled out of the attic, put Wiggles's dog coat on him, bundled up Lily and herself, and they went sledding. She towed Lily up and down the block, keeping in view of the house in case the furnace man arrived.

The flakes were still tumbling down and the snow now came past the ankles of Erin's boots. Lily was exuberant, but Erin was fraught with worry.

They went home and had nothing to warm them but the kitchen stove. The furnace man, rotund and whistling, arrived in the middle of supper and stayed in the basement for a troublingly short period of time.

"Well," Erin asked warily, "how long will it take to fix it?"

"Lady, I haven't seen a furnace like that in forty years," he said with a booming voice. "They quit making parts for those some time back."

She turned even colder. "That means I need a new one?"

"'Fraid so."

Erin must have looked particularly miserable, because he came over and patted her on the shoulder, promised to have it installed within twenty-four hours, and offered to let her pay it out by the month.

Grateful, Erin followed him out to his van where he apologized again for not being able to fix the furnace right away.

As she turned to go back into the house, she heard the scrape of a snow shovel. Wyatt was clearing the walk that led from the driveway to the house. He propped the shovel against a hedge and came toward her, stopping at the fence.

"Erin, I couldn't help but notice the repair truck. Is everything okay?" The reflected light from the snow partially illuminated his face.

Her stomach tightened. "Everything will be fine," she said.

"But what about tonight? I heard what he said."

"We'll be fine, Wyatt," she insisted. "We have sleeping bags and loads of blankets and there's always a motel."

He looked over her shoulder at her car, which sat under a pile of snow. Little of it was visible but the back bumper. "I don't think you're going anywhere in that."

She looked at him indignantly. "I wouldn't be so sure if I were you."

With a gloved hand, he grabbed one of the pickets of the fence and gave it a shake in frustration. "Erin, you can demonstrate your self-reliance tonight until your lips and your fingernails turn blue. But it's hardly necessary. You and Lily can stay in my house tonight and I'll go to a motel."

Her breath stalled in her chest. "I can't let you go to that kind of trouble."

"I don't need your permission," he said, reaching into his pocket, "just your cooperation." He dangled a set of keys in front of her. "Lily will enjoy the fireplace and Wiggles is welcome, too."

Erin knew that when it came to Lily's comfort, she couldn't say no. She took the keys and thanked him.

She finished the supper dishes, put what little they would both need in a backpack, and bundled Lily up in her red goosedown coat and bright yellow snow boots from the previous year. They barely fit. She tucked Wiggles in the crook of her arm and they set off, Lily kicking happily through the icy powder.

Erin let her ring the bell and almost instantly Wyatt appeared in the doorway, his hair still glistening from the snow. He wore corduroy jeans, hiking boots, and a heavy, gray fisherman's sweater.

He greeted Erin wordlessly, with a brief, mildly triumphant smile. He bent from the waist to address Lily.

"Hi, Peach," he teased, directing a wink toward Erin.

"Pumpkin," Lily corrected with a grin.

"I need to think of a name for you," he said, turning to Erin with a devilish gleam in his eye.

She bristled. "I'm sure a few have already come to mind."

He offered no response except for a faint smile.

Erin put Wiggles down and began to take off Lily's coat.

"Everything should be in order here at the Keegan bed and breakfast. There's only one drawback," he said. "There's only one bed—mine—but I welcome the opportunity to have two beautiful women in it at once."

Erin shot him a humorless look.

"Can Wiggles sleep in it too?" Lily asked.

"Most certainly," he said, taking Erin's coat and hanging it in the closet. "I even managed to change the sheets."

He led them into the living room where a golden fire crackled in the hearth. The room was cluttered with books and magazines. A necktie was flung over a chair, a pair of socks lay under a table, but it was deliciously, blessedly, and wonderfully warm.

"There's pizza in the freezer and spaghetti makings in the cabinet," he added, picking up his coat from the sofa. "Help yourselves."

Erin thanked him again, yet felt that the words were somehow inadequate.

"And now, I'll be off," he said with a wave. "Sweet dreams."

"Don't let the bedbug bite," Lily quipped.

Perversely, Erin's mood lifted. She suspected such things might not be unknown in one or two of Maple Springs's motels.

As the door closed behind him, she felt a twinge of guilt and something else as well. It was a vague and nagging sense of emptiness.

She and Lily had joined Wiggles in front of the fire, relishing its warmth, when a whirring noise sounded in the front of the house. She recognized it as the sound of tires spinning in the snow. She went to the window and found Wyatt's car at the end of the driveway, seemingly going nowhere. Then she remembered the sinkhole at the edge of the drive that the Swayzes could never seem to keep filled.

The wheels spun again, this time furiously. Erin reached for her coat, but before she could step outside, she heard Wyatt tramping heavily up the walk. She opened the door.

"I've got bad news," he said, with a final stamp of a snow-covered boot.

"You're stuck," she said. "Welcome to Vermont."

"I have even worse news," he said. "You're going to have to spend the night in my house—with me."

Erin swallowed hard. "I see," she said, a lull following. "Well, we could certainly make room for you in your own house."

He winked. "I was hoping you'd see it that way."

What Erin saw as an awkward situation Lily saw as a wonderful surprise. She had a puzzle. Could Wyatt help her with it? She could write her numbers. Did he want to see? The next thing Erin knew, it was almost ten, an hour past Lily's bedtime.

"But I'm not sleepy," she said with a yawn.

"Wyatt is," Erin said. "You've worn him out."

"Can I sleep on the sofa by the fire?"

"That's where I'm sleeping," Wyatt interjected.

"But you have a bed," Lily reasoned.

"Where's your Aunt Erin going to sleep?" Wyatt asked playfully. "The sofa isn't big enough for both of you."

"She can sleep in the bed with you."

Erin's cheeks tingled. She could feel his gaze on her before she caught sight of him studying her with slow and amused deliberation. "No, he can't," she said tersely.

Before Lily could ask any more questions, Erin whisked her off to bed.

"You must have set a record for tucking a kid in," Wyatt said a few minutes later, as she emerged from the bedroom.

"She was tired," Erin said defensively.

He cast her a sidelong glance. "I suppose you're going to tuck yourself in next."

"It's been a trying day."

"Apple cider might revive you a bit. Come on," he said

with an entreating look. ‘‘I was just going to heat some up.’’

Wyatt threw another log on the fire and disappeared into the kitchen. Erin, in her stocking feet, sat cross-legged on the sofa, staring into the dancing flames. Although only part of her wanted to, she couldn’t close the door on a man in his own house.

Wyatt emerged from the kitchen, handed her a steaming mug, and sat on the other side of the sofa. ‘‘You know, Erin, I don’t think that agreement we made to stay out of each other’s way is worth the paper it’s written on.’’

Erin’s fingers tightened around her cup. ‘‘I’m doing my best.’’

He studied her with lingering deliberation as the light from the fireplace flickered over the planes of his face. ‘‘I don’t doubt that you are.’’

‘‘And what about you?’’

He looked wistfully at the ceiling. ‘‘Oh, I toyed with the idea of letting you sit over there until your teeth chattered like castanets, but I’m too nice of a guy for that.’’

Erin’s mouth dropped open. ‘‘Listen to you. Shall I run and get a mirror so you can kiss it?’’

He removed the mug from her hand and set it down next to his. He rose quickly, pulling her up with him. ‘‘No, I’d rather kiss you.’’

Once his arms were around her, what little resistance she felt disappeared and she melted against him. He started with a brush of his lips against her neck, then a little kiss on the earlobe, making her veins feel like they were filled with champagne bubbles. Slowly, he nibbled his way up her cheekbone, then he kissed the tip of her nose, leaving her aching for more. Finally, his lips came down on hers with a hunger that surprised her.

Dazed by her own yearning, Erin touched his cheek, feeling along the plane of his rough jaw. Just underneath his chin, his pulse hammered under her fingertips. The kiss was filled with heat and fervor and, as Erin realized with a growing alarm, desire. It weakened her, and for an instant left her powerless, unable to break free of the force that held them together. After struggling with the conflicts inside her, she turned her face away and pulled back.

His eyes glistened with emotion and firelight as he held her at arm's length. "You can't run home this time."

"Maybe some other time," she said weakly.

He kissed her lightly, running his fingers through the silky strands of her hair. "Well, just maybe we're finally learning how to get along."

Erin blinked. How had it come to this, or was it even real? She heard the crackle of burning wood, felt its warmth, and saw the light and shadows that played across the room. But not until he pulled her into his arms again was she convinced that this was not a dream. For a while, they stood quietly with their arms around each other watching until the flames died.

Erin awoke to that peculiar brightness that snow brings. She was surprised that she had anything to awake from since it had seemed that sleep would never come. Beyond the closed bedroom door, she heard Lily's voice mingling unintelligibly with Wyatt's. Then she sat up abruptly. The reality of where she was and whose bed she'd been sleeping in hit her with full force. She smoothed her hair back from her face and took a deep breath. Staying here posed too much of a hazard to her emotions. She couldn't get home soon enough.

She dressed quickly in faded jeans, a blue shirt, and a

red Nordic ski sweater, hurriedly stuffing her nightgown into her backpack. She flicked a brush through her hair, splashed cold water on her face, and ran a toothbrush across her teeth.

But Lily was in no hurry to go anywhere. She and Wiggles were in the kitchen with Wyatt.

"Look, Aunt Erin, I can cook," Lily said, standing proudly by the toaster.

Erin kissed her briefly on the crown, then her eyes met Wyatt's. They glittered darkly with meaning, causing Erin's heart to bang against her ribs.

"Good morning," he said with a knowing smile. He wore jeans and a dark blue sweater and thick woolen socks. He was unshaven, yet that seemed to add to, rather than detract from, his undeniable appeal.

"Good morning," she said. She quickly shifted her gaze away, not daring to get lost in his eyes.

"You didn't tell me that little Lily here was such an early bird," he said. There was a hint of fatigue in his eyes.

"Seven isn't so early, is it?" Erin asked.

"Try five," Wyatt said, breaking an egg into a bowl. "I opened my eyes and there she was, standing right over me, looking me right in the face."

Erin gave Lily a look of disapproval. "Lily, that's not like you."

"I wasn't sleepy," she said. "I thought it was later."

"Well, that's understandable, but I think you should apologize to Wyatt for staring at him while he was sleeping."

The corner of her mouth turned down. "I'm sorry," she drawled.

Wyatt ruffled her bangs. "It's all right. Now, how about a scrambled egg?"

"Wyatt, really," Erin interjected, "you don't have to . . ."

"What's wrong? Don't you trust my cooking?"

"No, but that's not the issue."

"It doesn't matter what the issue is. Eggs I can do."

And he could. They were cooked just right—firm, yet with a little gloss remaining. And the sausages, the heat-and-serve kind, didn't leave much room for failure. Lily even managed not to burn the toast.

Lily ate happily, cleaning her plate by herself, except for the bite of sausage she gave Wiggles. But Erin ate only with great effort. She was confused and uncertain and she feared her better instincts were failing her, that she was losing control over her heart. There they were in a scene of pleasant domesticity and for an instant, she'd savored it, just as she'd savored Wyatt's kisses.

"And now, Lily," Wyatt said, getting up, "I'm going to make magic toast. Have you ever heard of magic toast?"

Lily, still in her gown, shook her head, her dark hair swinging back and forth.

He plucked a remaining piece of toast out of the toaster and placed it on a cutting board. He took it to the counter. "Now, you can't see it until I'm finished."

Erin watched as he grabbed a jar of red preserves out of the refrigerator and a small knife out of a drawer. The movement of his broad shoulders suggested that something interesting was indeed taking place. A moment later, he turned and presented Lily with a heart topped with red jam.

The child's eyes widened in delight.

"The maid did things like that for my sister and me," he explained to Erin. "My father was always at the factory and my mother was heaven knows where. I think she felt a bit sorry for us."

Touched, Erin kissed his beard-shadowed cheek. The kiss was punctuated by the ring of the telephone.

Wyatt, keeping his eyes on Erin, grabbed the receiver off the wall a few feet away. ''Yes, George,'' he said with a tone of familiarity. His gaze shifted to nowhere in particular. ''We should be ready to start proceedings when I get back to Boston. . . . Yes, I know it's going to be a tough case. . . . Keep me posted. . . . I'll see you in a few weeks.''

December would come and Wyatt would go. The brief happiness that Erin had been foolish enough to feel vanished like Lily's heart-shaped toast.

Chapter Eight

Erin, wrapped in a patchwork quilt, sat in front of her computer screen listening to the banging and hammering of the furnace men in the basement and to the uneasy beating of her own heart. When a woman never wanted to leave a man's arms, it could only mean one thing. And the night before, she'd wanted to stay in Wyatt's forever.

She pulled the quilt more tightly around her as if to shield herself from a realization too painful to contemplate. She couldn't love Wyatt Keegan. He would have shattered her life and Lily's if he could have. And now that he'd become part of their existence in a way she'd never dreamed, he'd soon be walking out of their lives just as easily as he'd walked in, and with his heart still under lock and key.

She looked through the doorway into the living room where Lily, bundled in her red coat and striped mittens, played with her dolls. She was too little to have had such big hurts. A pain riveted Erin's heart. She'd never felt so incapable of protecting her.

Suddenly, the air was pierced by a screech and a clang, followed by the sound of heavy footsteps. The furnace man appeared in her doorway, wiping his forehead with the back of his hand.

"We're ready to haul 'er out," he announced. "If it's

all right with you, we'll move some of the furniture back a bit.''

Grateful for the diversion, Erin got up from her desk. ''That will be fine, Mr. Finley.''

She and Lily stood back as three workers maneuvered the hulk of rusting metal through the house. A glance at the thermostat showed it was forty degrees inside.

''You got some interesting things down in that basement,'' Mr. Finley said as he came back through the door. ''I saw a statue like that once in a museum.''

''Oh, that,'' Erin said with an embarrassed laugh. It was a replica of Michelangelo's *David*. ''It was for a client who later changed his mind. I just sort of stuck it behind the furnace.''

He gave a little shrug and a laugh. ''Well, we may have to ask him to move over some.''

Erin nodded. ''It's not that heavy. It's not real marble.''

A few hours later, a shiny new furnace sat in the basement under the contemplative watch of the statue. Upstairs, Erin threw off the quilt, unzipped Lily's coat, removed Wiggles's cape, and together they basked in its warmth.

The ring of the telephone brought her to her feet again. It was Wyatt. Her heart jumped at the deep timbre of his voice.

''Is everything okay? Do you have heat now?'' His tone was almost businesslike.

When she assured him that everything was in order, he seemed satisfied. The colleague who had taken him to work brought him home, and the car, with the help of a wrecker, was now unstuck. She thanked him once again and he hung up, with little acknowledgment of what had passed between them the night before. She was left with an ache that penetrated to her bones.

* * *

The sun reappeared a few days later, reducing to a lump a snowman that she and Lily had made. For days, she heard nothing from Wyatt. His house remained dark and the driveway stayed empty long into the night.

She threw herself into her work with extra zeal, as she always did when she was troubled. She couldn't get Wyatt out of her thoughts but she did locate an antique Shaker table that had been eluding her for months and she even managed to find a possible buyer for the statue. A decorator in New York was redoing an Italian-style villa. The owner was doing some business upstate and could take a little detour and come by and look at it on Saturday.

In the meantime, she kept Lily busy as well. She dropped her off for several afternoons at the store with Tabitha and let her spend a morning with a preschool classmate.

On Saturday morning, she was cleaning up after breakfast when Lily ran into the kitchen, her eyes wide. "Aunt Erin, there's a big car outside. A b-i-g car," she said, holding her arms out to her sides.

"That's probably the statue man," she explained. She snapped the dishwasher closed and dried her hands. The bell rang as she hurried toward the door.

Two men stood on the front porch. One tall and one short, they were dressed in black overcoats and black fedoras and wore dark glasses. Behind them was a black stretch limousine with darkened windows.

"Yes?" she said, standing cautiously behind the partially opened door.

"Miss March?"

Erin nodded.

"We're here to see the statue," one said with a heavy Brooklyn accent. A large diamond on his pinkie ring twinkled as he rolled an unlit cigar between his thumb and forefinger.

Erin forced a smile and swallowed. ''Oh, yes, of course. It's in the basement. Please come in.''

They entered in single file, the short one with the cigar leading the tall one. His alligator shoes squeaked as he walked. He paused and took off his hat, revealing well-oiled black hair. The glasses stayed on.

''I've been collecting fake statues to put around my swimming pool,'' he explained. ''The real stuff I keep in the house. Creates a big impression, ya know?''

''It certainly does.''

Lily, wide-eyed and wearing a milk mustache, stepped close beside her.

''Cute little girl ya got there,'' he said. He bent down from the waist to address Lily. ''How'd ya like a present?''

Uncharacteristically, Lily pressed in closer to Erin.

''A shy one, huh?'' he said. He whipped a gold money clip from his pocket and peeled off a twenty-dollar bill.

''Oh, I couldn't let you give her that,'' Erin protested.

''Believe me, it's nothin','' he said. ''She can go get herself some little trinket.''

Erin tried to give it back but he refused it.

''Now, for that statue,'' he said.

Just as she turned to lead them into the basement, the doorbell rang. ''Excuse me,'' she said, taking Lily's hand. ''I have to get the door.''

Wyatt, his brow creased, stood on the porch, his green gaze seeming to reach down into her. Her heart knocked against her ribs.

''I know you're busy, but I'll wait,'' he said. ''May I come in?''

She stepped back as Lily fidgeted in excitement. "Yes, I'm just going to show these gentlemen a statue."

Wyatt addressed them courteously but his demeanor was somewhat stern. Then he followed them to the basement where the statue stood scowling at the furnace from underneath its cap of stony curls.

The short man rapped his knuckles against the replica and perused it in the dim basement light without removing his dark glasses. Wyatt watched both of them through assessing eyes.

"I'll take him," he said with a wave of his cigar.

Upstairs, he gave Erin an assortment of bills and they agreed on shipping arrangements. It was to go to him personally, Mr. Luigi Bartello. Nervous, Erin filled out the receipt as quickly as possible. They all watched as the men left in a long, black streak.

Wyatt quickly turned to Erin with his hands thrust into his pockets. One eyebrow was raised in skepticism.

"Having the mob over for tea?"

Her cheeks tingled. "We're both supposed to mind our own affairs, remember?

He swiftly took her by the shoulders. His face was within inches of hers, his gaze intense. "How could I not notice anything like a stretch limo idling at the curb? How could I just sit still and let those thugs march into your house?"

Her color deepened. "Have you ever thought about moving your chair away from that window?"

His nostrils flared in anger as his fingers tightened around her shoulders. "Good grief, Erin. We're not talking about two Benedictine monks here. One day I look out and see what appears to be a witch driving a sports car; next, it's the Mafia, or so it seems. You don't do business with those characters, do you?"

Erin looked at him incredulously. "Of course not. I mean only one of them and just this once."

"That man gave me some money," Lily interjected in a singsong voice. She held up the crisp bill for Wyatt to see.

His arms dropped from Erin's shoulders. He took the bill from Lily and examined it closely, holding it up to the light, then gave it back to her with a scowl.

"I know," Erin said, anticipating what he was going to say next. "There's no telling where that came from. I tried to discourage him, but those aren't the kind of people you want to pressure."

Wyatt looked at her for a moment, then a lopsided smile slowly appeared on his face.

Her heart thumped as she looked into his eyes.

"Look, I can't help it," he said with a shrug. "I'm honestly trying to mind my own business. And haven't I done a good job of it the last week or so?"

Erin nodded.

"So what do you want me to do when Atilla the Hun rides up on his horse," he asked, "ignore him?"

"Oh, Wyatt," she groaned. "He won't be coming. He's dead."

His expression stiffened but there was a twinkle in his eyes. "Won't you take this seriously?"

"Of course. It's just that in this business you encounter all sorts. When I worked in Boston, I met a dethroned prince once. He wanted some rare stained glass. We almost never found it."

She caught a tinge of impatience in his expression. "Erin, I don't think our agreement is working. I'm not even sure I want it to work and I don't think you're sure either."

She stared at him, in silence.

"I care about you and Lily," he said, a touch of color appearing along his cheekbones. "I'm sorry if I seem to barge in when I'm not especially wanted. Call it a protective instinct or whatever, but it's hard to ignore. Can't we just be friends?"

Erin felt a painful twist in her heart. For her, it was too late. Her feelings had gone beyond friendship, far beyond her own understanding. Worse yet, they were for a man unwilling to take another chance on love. But she was determined that she wouldn't have to endure the additional pain of his knowing. She held out a hand and hoped that he couldn't feel the trembling she felt inside.

"Friends, then," she said, managing a smile.

His gaze lingered over her face as he took her hand. His grasp was firm and heated. "Friends," he said.

Friends or not, Erin was concerned over what Wyatt might really be thinking. He didn't understand that it was perfectly safe to be out on Halloween night in Maple Springs. And yes, she'd had some odd visitors, but they'd been harmless, except for the Mafia characters, and she wouldn't have let them come if she'd known. Her life must indeed look strange to a man who was accustomed to order and predictability. But surely he could see that she was doing the best she could and that Lily was thriving. But she was afraid he would never be completely convinced that he'd been wrong about her.

She deliberated about this while Lily was in the kitchen playing with a mound of potter's clay. Another Saturday had rolled around. She'd seen Wyatt only in passing. He'd been busy getting ready for a court date and had also spent several days in Boston on a business trip. In the meantime, she'd been trying, without success, to block out the intimate moments they'd shared. But she couldn't forget the warm harbor of his embrace and the teasing way his lips moved over her throat and her face.

Lily poked and squeezed at a piece of clay that looked remotely like a dog while Wiggles lay stretched out on the braided rug in front of the sink. There were streaks of clay on Lily's face, in her hair, and on the front of her sweatshirt.

Erin was watching, trying to pull herself together enough to put the living room back in order, when she heard a car door slam. She went to a living-room window, stepping around a dollhouse and its scattered furniture along the way, and pulled back the curtain. A black Mercedes sat in the driveway. She inwardly groaned. She didn't need any more mysterious visitors, any more strange men in dark glasses. What was Wyatt going to think now?

But the mystery was quickly solved when a tall, blond man emerged from the driver's side. A dark-haired woman appeared on the other side of the car. Erin turned cold and stepped back from the window. It was Mallory and Yale Holbrooke.

Her heart lurching, Erin dashed into the kitchen, leaping over the dollhouse. ''Erin, your Aunt Mallory and Uncle Yale are here,'' she said breathlessly. ''Let's hurry and get cleaned up.''

Her mind was wracked with questions as she quickly wiped the clay from Lily's face and hands. Why had they come now and why unannounced? Why had they waited so long to see Lily? The doorbell rang before she could finish getting Lily out of her soiled sweatshirt. Wiggles began to bark. She rushed Lily to her room and quickly pulled the shirt over her head. The bell rang again.

"Oh, dear," she said, her heart racing faster than her fingers could move.

She finished pulling a clean, red sweatshirt over the child's head just as the bell rang a third time. She smoothed down Lily's hair and her own and rushed to the door.

Rattled and wearing faded jeans and a old gray rag sweater which had almost worn through at the elbows, Erin was a contrast to the composed couple in expensive overcoats standing on the front porch.

"Mallory and Yale," she said, trying to sound as gracious as she could, "what a surprise. Please come in."

"How are you, Erin?" Mallory asked in a cultivated tone.

"Very well, thank you," she said, stepping aside.

"And Lily?"

"You can see for yourself," she said, turning. But Lily wasn't there. Erin's heart thumped. "Please take off your coats and sit down," she said, motioning toward the antique coatrack inside the small entry. "I'll get her."

Erin found her watching from around the dining-room door. She was holding Wiggles.

"Lily, come and greet your aunt and uncle," she said, placing a hand on the child's shoulder.

When Lily entered the room, Mallory bent her tall, willowy form from the waist and looked at her as if she were inspecting a piece of art. "Look at that, Yale," she said finally. "She's her mother all over again."

Erin saw Lily as a tiny version of her father, but this wasn't an argument to be raised here and now.

"How are you, sweetie?" she continued.

"Fine," she said softly.

She touched a perfectly manicured finger to Lily's dark crown. "Oh, my, what have you got in your hair?"

''Dirt,'' Lily responded.

Erin quickly explained the pottery project.

''I see,'' Mallory said, seemingly disinterested. ''Why don't you put the dog down and let me hold you in my lap?''

Lily's mouth quirked in reluctance as she released Wiggles from her arms. When she did, the little dog began to bark at the guests. Erin held him in her arm to quiet him.

Mallory, dressed in nubby black silk pants and a tailored white silk blouse, sat in the wicker rocker and pulled Lily onto her lap. The child looked mildly uncomfortable.

''Perhaps we should apologize for dropping in like this,'' Yale said, ''but with things being less formal in the country, we didn't think you would mind.''

''You're welcome anytime,'' she said, trying to sound relaxed. Keeping the dog with her, she sat down on the opposite side of the sofa from Yale.

''Wyatt said that Lily is quite something,'' Mallory said. ''I just had to see for myself.''

Erin felt a stab of alarm at the mention of Wyatt's name. Had she been wrong to even begin to trust him? Trying to ignore the growing sense of unease spreading through her, she listed some of Lily's activities and accomplishments, from preschool to helping Tabitha at the store.

''Wonderful,'' Mallory said, giving Lily a squeeze. ''But it's too bad there's not much in the way of cultural opportunities for her here. You know—ballet lessons and such.'' She cast a critical glance toward Lily's red high-top sneakers and frowned.

''Nothing is perfect,'' Erin said, managing a slight smile.

Mallory put Lily's hands in hers. ''Least of all these little fingernails.''

Erin looked at the tiny, dark crescents of clay under each one and cringed inwardly. Quickly, she reminded Mallory how they got there.

Mallory responded with a patronizing smile. "In the country I guess it doesn't matter so much."

Her cheeks warming, Erin said nothing. Instead, she politely excused herself to prepare a tray of tea and cookies. But in the kitchen, she chewed the inside of her cheek in indignation. What was Mallory trying to say, that Lily's life wasn't what it could have been in Boston? She took a long, slow breath from the depths of her lungs, then exhaled raggedly. She was giving Lily everything she needed, everything that really mattered. She worked hard, sacrificed, and gave Lily her best. She could do no more.

As she waited for the tea to steep, she could hear the Holbrookes questioning Lily. The questions were friendly, but they only added to Erin's anxiety. Did she like preschool? Who were her friends? Could she ride a bicycle yet? What were some of the things she liked to do?

Erin propped her mouth into the best smile she could manage before she entered the living room with the tea.

"Lily says she likes going to the park with you and the dog," Yale said as she set the tray on the coffee table.

Erin smiled at Lily, who fidgeted on Mallory's lap. She scooted forward to get down, but Mallory pulled her back.

"We go for walks every day," she explained, reaching for Lily's hand. "It's a special time we have together, when we can talk about things. It started out for Wiggles's benefit, but all of us enjoy it."

Lily climbed onto the sofa next to Wiggles. Erin handed her a teacup filled with a milk and tea mixture and served her a cookie. She sat next to the child and the dog.

"I'm sorry we haven't done a better job of keeping in touch," Mallory said, tossing her sleek, shoulder-length hair back slightly. Earrings with the unmistakable look of gold glowed on her earlobes. "Our careers have kept us so tied up that we haven't had time to leave the city. But I do think about Lily quite a lot, and I hope she has enjoyed the gifts we've sent."

"You have, haven't you, Lily?" Erin asked, turning toward the little girl.

Lily, wearing a milk mustache, nodded. "Thank you."

Erin smiled at her gratefully for the unprompted display of manners.

"Wyatt probably told you that we're starting a second business," Yale said. "How's your business coming along?"

Erin's fingers tightened around her cup. "Fine," she said, exaggerating slightly. "It's growing."

His eyes narrowed as if her assessment was insufficient. "It's a challenge, I'm sure. Any business is, especially a new one."

"Of course," Erin said uneasily

"Well, dear," Mallory said, pulling up her cuff to reveal a gold watch, "we really should be going if we're going to get back in time to go to the theater."

Yale rose. "We really should."

They stood in the entry while Erin got their coats. Wiggles jumped down from the sofa and sniffed at Mallory's black suede pumps. Then he jumped up and put his front paws on her pant leg.

"You're a pesky little thing, aren't you?" she said, swatting him away. "You'd better not snag my pants. My personal shopper spent days finding these."

Erin, holding both coats, commanded him to stay. The little dog sat down by the door.

Mallory turned to Erin as Yale helped her with her coat. "I'm sorry for popping in like this without notice, but I got a sudden whim to see Lily. I can't get over how she's grown."

"Two years is a long time in a child's life," Erin said.

Suddenly, the air became almost palpable with what was left unsaid. Since the judge's decision, few words had been exchanged between them, until now.

Yale cleared his throat awkwardly, then reached down and picked up Lily. "It's time to say good-bye to your Uncle Yale."

As he held her, Wiggles rose on hind legs and put his front paws on Yale's pant leg and gave a little yap. Mallory quickly opened the door, and before Erin could respond, she pushed the dog out to the front porch with her foot and closed the door.

"Wiggles!" Lily cried, scrambling out of Yale's arms.

Erin pulled her back. "Say good-bye to your Aunt Mallory and I'll get Wiggles and put him in the backyard."

She threw on her coat and stepped out onto the porch, but the little dog wasn't there. Her heart gave an uneasy thump. But before she had a chance to check the rest of the yard, the Holbrookes exited the house with Lily. Each gave Erin a brief handshake.

Waving good-bye, they got into the Mercedes. They were hardly out of the driveway when Lily broke into a run toward the backyard. Erin followed.

Breathlessly, Lily appeared at the gate. "Aunt Erin, where's Wiggles?"

Her stomach tightened. "I don't know, but try not to worry. He couldn't have gone far."

Lily took off running to the other side of the house. ‘‘Wig-gles!’’ she called.

They looked under the porch, under the car, and in the garage. They looked in the house again, but there was no sign of him. Lily’s eyes brimmed with tears.

‘‘He may be at Wyatt’s,’’ she said, trying to sound encouraging. ‘‘Let’s go see.’’

Wyatt was the last person she wanted to see at that moment. She was so confused and upset over the possibility that he might be connected to the visit in some negative way that she was on the verge of tears. But she had to see him. Her hand trembled as she rang the doorbell.

He was the picture of perfect calm when he opened the door. He had a law book in one hand and reading glasses resting on top his head.

But Erin, her heart wrenching, was gnawing her lower lip.

His eyes narrowed. ‘‘Is something wrong?’’

‘‘Wyatt, we can’t find Wiggles,’’ she managed to say, her voice tight. ‘‘Have you seen him?’’

‘‘No, I haven’t seen anything,’’ he said. ‘‘I’ve been in the dining room getting ready for a case.’’ He laid his book down on a small table in the entry and put his glasses on top. He grabbed a parka out of the closet. ‘‘I’ll help you look.’’

‘‘No, it’s not necessary,’’ she protested.

‘‘Maybe not,’’ he said firmly, ‘‘but I’m going anyway.’’

They canvassed Wyatt’s yard, then Erin’s again, but the little dog couldn’t be found. Lily burst into tears.

Wyatt picked her up and held her close, kissing her dark bangs. With his other arm, he pulled Erin close, his thumb flicking over the nape of her neck and sending little rivulets of sensation down her spine. Her yearning for him was overshadowed by the harsh reminder the afternoon had brought: he still worked for the Holbrookes. What were they up to?

"How did the little guy get out?" he asked.

Erin explained briefly.

His eyes widened at the mention of the Holbrookes, but he said nothing. "Come on," he said finally, his arm dropping from her shoulder. "Let's take a walk through the neighborhood. He's bound to turn up."

But he didn't. Wyatt, alternately leading Lily and carrying her, worked one side of the street while Erin searched the other. They walked through alleys and through adjoining streets. Dusk began to fall and Erin was sick with worry. Not only was Wiggles missing, but she was haunted by the nature of the Holbrookes' surprise visit. Why had they waited until now to come?

The visit brought back the raw and elemental fear that they might again attempt to take her. Chances of their succeeding were slim, but they could bring trouble and disharmony into their lives.

Erin went from door to door, knocking on each one as the light faded. Everyone was sympathetic and promised to keep watch, but there was still no Wiggles. The temperature began to fall as her fears began to rise. How could he have just vanished into thin air? Perhaps he'd been stolen. And without the right shelter, he could suffer frostbite or worse on a frigid night.

She crossed the street toward Wyatt who was coming toward her from the steps of an old Colonial house. Lily was resting in the crook of his arm, her face swollen from crying. Erin, her heart aching, reached out to take her.

"No luck," she said.

"None here, either," Wyatt said ruefully. "Let's take Lily home and get our bearings."

Even a pizza, which Wyatt ordered out, did little to elevate Lily's mood. She barely ate one slice.

"Stay home, give her a hot bath, and put her to bed," he said, rising from the table. "I'll go out and look some more."

Erin's heart gave a little twist. "Wyatt, I can't ask you to do that."

"You don't have to," he said, reaching for his coat. "Case closed."

And with little more than a good-bye, he was gone into the dark and frigid night.

Erin did everything she could to reassure Lily as she put her to bed. They would do everything possible to find Wiggles. He had a tag with his address and phone number, didn't he? And no, Aunt Mallory didn't mean for Wiggles to run away from home.

As Erin turned out the light in Lily's room, her thoughts about Mallory were less charitable than her words. She wanted to do something to her, with strangulation coming first to mind. A pox, or, better still, moths, on the Holbrookes' designer clothes.

The next few hours seemed to stretch into eternity. Despite the efficient hum of the new furnace, Erin felt chilled. She sat in the wicker rocker with a magazine on her lap but her mind continually darted from the pages to Wyatt and the troubling events of the day. Poor Wiggles. He was so tiny and unaccustomed to staying outdoors in the cold for long periods of time. If something happened to him, Lily's heart would be broken.

Erin went to the window and saw the branches of the

old maple bowing in the wind. Wyatt's coat appeared sufficient, but he'd worn nothing on his head and he hadn't been wearing gloves. Erin's heart twisted with guilt as she thought of the icy wind racing through his hair.

This was the man she'd fallen in love with—the man who went out of his way to do things for herself and Lily. She loved the way he had sat uncomfortably, yet amused, in a child-sized chair. She loved the way his lopsided smile melted her troubles away. She loved the fervor of his embrace. Yesterday, he was someone she'd learned to trust and forgive, but tonight, after the Holbrookes' visit, she wasn't sure who he was. That left a hollow ache in the center of her heart.

Footsteps sounded on the front porch and her heart leaped into her throat. She opened the door to find Wyatt, his hair and shoulders flecked with sleet.

"Oh, Wyatt," she said as he stepped inside.

His gaze met hers in a sort of frozen futility as he held out two empty hands, two very red and cold-stiffened hands. "I'm sorry, Erin," he said, rubbing his palms together and trying to flex his fingers. But he seemed barely able to bend them. "I searched every street and alley I could."

She felt a crumpling sensation of loss not only for Lily and Wiggles but for Wyatt. "I appreciate what you did. Come in and warm up. I'll make you some hot chocolate."

"No argument here," he said, brushing the moisture from his hair. He fumbled with the snaps on his coat but his fingers were too stiff to negotiate them easily. Erin, her pulse racing, reached up and began pulling the snaps apart for him, then she took both of his hands in hers.

They were so cold that the chill coursed through her own body.

Their gazes fused. Alarmed at the intensity of her feelings, she quickly turned away. She hung up his coat and he followed her into the kitchen.

"I feel like all this is partly my fault," he said, sitting at the table. His face, reddened by the cold, held a pained expression.

Erin swallowed hard. "What do you mean?"

"I encouraged the Holbrookes to visit you and Lily, to try to make peace, so to speak. If they hadn't come, this wouldn't have happened."

She looked at him numbly over her shoulder as she took cups out of the cabinet. "You wanted them to make peace?"

"Yes. I don't think that's a bad idea, do you?"

Erin set the cups down with a clatter. "They frightened me, Wyatt," she said, her voice unsteady. "You frighten me."

He rose to his feet and came toward her. "What on earth are you talking about?"

"I had a feeling they were here on a witch-hunt."

He took her by the shoulders. "Erin," he said, shaking his head and looking deeply into her eyes, "I only suggested to them that they bury the hatchet. This case is over as far as I'm concerned."

Her eyes brimmed with tears. "I thought it was over until you came."

He pulled her into his arms. "It's all right," he whispered into her ear. He held her so close that she could feel his heart beating strongly against his chest. His hands followed the outline of her shoulders and her throat. They moved up to her cheeks, touching them so lightly that the chill in his fingers was barely discernible. His lips touched hers for one fleeting moment. Then, suddenly, he released her, leaving her yearning for more.

"We'll work all this out," he said, his voice thick with emotion. "We'll part as friends, I promise."

As she nodded, a dull ache settled in her chest. She wanted more than just a friendship with Wyatt Keegan, but it was clear that she would never have his love.

Chapter Nine

After a night of fitful sleep, Erin was awakened by the ringing of the doorbell. Her heart skittered as she scrambled out of bed. She threw on her robe and rushed toward the door, the cold floor biting the soles of her feet. The light coming through the living-room windows barely hinted of dawn.

Erin fumbled with the deadbolt lock as the bell rang once again. She flipped on the porch light and opened the door. On the front porch stood Mrs. Stahl. In her arm was the Yorkshire terrier.

"Wiggles!" Erin cried with a rush of joy. She took the little dog from the neighbor and held him tightly. He licked her face excitedly. "Oh, thank goodness. I'm so relieved. Where did you find him?"

Mrs. Stahl placed a wrinkled hand apologetically over her chest and gave an embarrassed smile. "In my garage. I'm so sorry, but I must have shut him in by accident. You see, I just took in a stray cat and I'm keeping him in the garage so my Felix won't get too upset. You know how jealous pets can be. Well, anyway, I had the garage door open yesterday for a short time while I was carrying in a few bags of groceries. Well, Wiggles must have come in to meet the cat and to investigate. There's cat food and a kitty basket in there. Not seeing him, I closed the garage door. This morning, when I went out to feed the cat and check on him, Wiggles came running out. I'm just awfully sorry."

"It's all right, Mrs. Stahl," Erin said, stroking the dog's long, silky coat. "All's well that ends well. Lily will be so happy."

"Sorry to awaken you, dear, but I thought you'd want to know as soon as possible. And you tell Lily that we'll spend an afternoon making doll clothes."

Erin thanked her once again and, with an audible sigh of relief, closed the door. She set the dog down and he made a beeline for Lily's room. She followed him and found Lily sitting up in bed, her eyes wide with disbelief, then joy. "Wiggles!" she squealed.

Erin's heart sprouted wings as she watched the happy reunion. Erin explained briefly how he was found, but Lily seemed too taken in by the moment to listen.

The dog was so excited that he refused his bowl of fresh food and gave his water only a quick lap. Lily, wearing a long flannel nightgown, swooped him up and danced out of the kitchen. Erin dressed quickly in flannel-lined jeans and an oversized white fisherman's sweater, but as she gave the laces on one of her hiking boots a final tug, she heard the front door open.

"I'm going to tell Wyatt," Lily called excitedly.

Before Erin could respond, she heard the front door slam shut. She stepped into her other boot, and without taking time to lace it properly, tied it and rushed after her.

"Lily, wait," she yelled, running down the front steps.

But it was too late. At that moment, Lily, wearing only her nightgown and red high-top sneakers, was at Wyatt's, ringing the doorbell before Erin caught up with her. Breathless, she put the dog down and picked Lily up to keep her warm. "Lily, wait," she whispered. "It's not even seven o'clock. And look at you. You've run off without your coat."

But she couldn't undo what had been done and now they couldn't just walk away. After a moment, when Erin had concluded with some relief that Wyatt had slept through the bell, she turned to leave. They were only a few steps away when she heard the door click open. She whirled about to find Wyatt, barefoot and dressed in a dark robe, standing in the doorway. Wiggles scampered up to him. Wyatt squinted, then rubbed his eyes as if he were uncertain of what he was seeing.

"We found him!" Lily cried. Erin held her tightly to keep her from running to him.

Wyatt bent down and picked him up and a slow smile spread across his face. "You've got a lot of explaining to do, Wiggles." The dog, who looked even smaller against Wyatt's chest, panted happily.

"He got all locked up in Mrs. Stahl's garage, all night long," Lily said.

Wyatt, his face covered with stubble, ran a hand through his tousled hair and looked at Erin, sending a current of longing through her.

"Wyatt, I'm sorry. We didn't mean to get you up. Lily was so excited that she was at your door before I could catch her."

A sparkling warmth appeared in his sleep-shrouded eyes. "I like having women beating down my door. Just tell me this is real and not a dream."

"It's real."

"You'd better come in then," he said, touching her elbow. "Real women get cold."

She set Lily down in the entry and he handed the child

the dog. Erin briefly told him the story, barely able to keep her eyes off the V of dark hair at the throat of his robe.

"Wyatt, you were wonderful to help us look. I don't know how to thank you."

He ran a hand over a bearded cheek and looked at her like a man tempted by a freshly baked cake. "I have an idea."

In the moment of silence that followed, her heart gave a sound knock against her rib cage.

"You can give me a cooking lesson and show me how to sew on a button like you promised."

Erin released the breath she was holding. "It's done."

The cooking lesson was that evening. Erin worked to keep it simple. She assembled ingredients for meat loaf, rounded up some large baking potatoes, and bought heads of fresh broccoli and cauliflower. She got apples to bake for dessert. For now, that would be enough of a challenge for a man at the eggs and toast level.

He arrived shaven and smelling faintly of cedar and the Vermont outdoors. He peered down at Erin from underneath a shock of hair that had fallen across his forehead and presented her with a bottle of wine.

"It's customary to bring the teacher an apple, but why not grapes?"

She'd barely taken the bottle and thanked him when Lily came bounding through the living room with Wiggles at her heels. Lily was dressed in her customary overalls. Wiggles wore a purple bandanna. Wyatt hooked his hands under her arms and hoisted her into the air. She giggled excitedly. Erin felt a grinding ache under her heart, knowing this would all soon come to an end.

Wyatt was a quick study: With the sleeves of his red

flannel shirt rolled up to his elbows, he chopped, sliced, and mixed, under Erin's supervision. Lily sat at the kitchen table with a coloring book and crayons, doing more watching than coloring. And the looks she gave Wyatt were nothing short of hero worship. They were looks that made Erin's insides crumple like burning paper.

With a triumphant flourish, he put the meat loaf, the potatoes, and the apples in the oven and leaned against the counter, crossing one ankle over another. "You know, Erin," he said, folding his arms over his chest, "I never thought it would come to this. Here I am in a backwater Vermont village baking meat loaf and liking it."

Her spirits rose.

"But Boston, as my grandmother used to think of it, is the hub of the universe. It's always been the hub of my universe, anyway. I like looking out my office window and seeing all the activity outside. Ever hear of genetic memory?" he asked.

Erin shook her head.

"Those who believe in it say it's a sense of place that passes down through the genes. It's that odd yearning for the city or the country of your ancestors, a feeling of kinship with your surroundings. It's an ingrained sense of belonging. Sound strange?"

"No," she said softly. "That's the way I feel about Vermont."

He bit his lower lip and looked at her wistfully, as if he wanted to say something, but he didn't.

Feeling an aching sense of loss, she turned to wipe a counter that had already been wiped clean.

"Aunt Erin?" Lily said, breaking the lull.

"Yes, Lily," she said, turning.

"Can I give Wyatt my picture now?"

Erin's stomach tightened. It was the drawing that she had hoped Lily would forget about. "Yes," she answered. She could hardly say anything else.

The little girl went skipping off to her room and returned with the brightly crayoned art. "Here, Wyatt, I made this just for you."

He took the oversized sheet, lavishly praising the drawings of himself, Erin, Lily, and Wiggles in front of the saltbox house. In the picture, one of his arms and one of his shoes were bigger than the other and the house listed to the left, but he told her it was "perfect."

To Erin, it was a perfect illustration of how perfectly complicated things had gotten.

Wyatt's eyes caught Erin's in one fleeting and knowing moment, jolting her. His jaw tensed. Whatever he was thinking, she didn't want him to get the idea that she was encouraging Lily's fantasies.

"Lily, put the picture in the living room until it's time for Wyatt to go," she said.

A silence fell as Lily dashed out of the room.

"Children have their own way of looking at things," she said finally. "They're often unrealistic."

He smiled sadly but said nothing.

The meal was a success, such a success that Lily, with a full stomach and a deficit of sleep from the night before, fell asleep on the sofa shortly afterwards. Wyatt carried her to bed and Erin tucked her in, placing her teddy bear next to her. Wiggles curled up on the other side.

As Erin turned out the light, Wyatt slipped his arm around her shoulders. "There are some things I want to tell you," he said, closing the door to Lily's room.

She tensed, thinking of the familylike portrait Lily had

drawn. "I know what you're going to say," she said, pulling away from him, "and you don't need to say it."

He shook his head. "You *don't* know what I'm going to say. Come on. Come sit down."

Putting herself at as much distance as possible, Erin sat dismally in the rocker and watched as he poured two glasses of wine. She should throw him out in the cold for all the grief he had caused her.

He handed her a glass and then had the gall to smile.

"Erin," he said, sitting across from her, "I think you're doing wonderfully with Lily. She's spirited, to be sure, but the two of you are kindred spirits and the bond between you is something to behold. Even the most hardened heart couldn't not be moved by it."

A lump rose in Erin's throat. Yes, she loved Lily more than anything, but what else was he trying to tell her?

His expression darkened. "Once the Holbrookes learned that I was living next door to you and Lily, they began to ask a lot of questions. They were curious about your financial status, about Lily's behavior, about your personal life. I didn't tell them anything, Erin, except that you were both fine and that they should try to rebuild the relationship.

"When they asked me to represent them two years ago, I believed that they would be the best parents for Lily. If I didn't, I wouldn't have taken the case. But I no longer believe that."

Erin sat forward in her chair, too stunned to say anything.

Wyatt refilled their glasses. "The fact that they've had almost no role in her life in the last two years speaks for itself."

"Couldn't they again try to take her?" she asked.

"They could always try," he said, "but under the present circumstances, there are no grounds. Besides, no judge would dare part the two of you. It would be like taking Bambi from its mother.''

Erin laughed, then began to cry, crazy tears that didn't make any sense. Wyatt got up, took her glass from her hand, and set it aside. He pulled her up out of the chair and took her into his arms. She melted against him, soaking the front of his sweater.

''Sorry,'' she said, with an embarrassed sniff. She pulled away, dabbing at his chest with her loose shirttail.

He slipped his hands up her back, just above her waist, and caressed it. She gasped as the heat of his fingers ignited her nerve endings, sending dizzying signals to her brain.

''I'm sorry, too,'' he murmured into her hair. ''I'm sorry I called you a gadabout, a mere girl, someone who didn't know what she was getting into, and for anything else I might have said.''

She raised her chin and smiled at him through her tears. He responded with a lopsided, but somewhat melancholy, grin, then touched his lips to hers. His fingers played along her spine as the kiss deepened, taking her breath away. His mouth moved over hers with possession and longing. Then he abruptly pulled away.

She looked at him, confused, her heart thundering. His eyes were murky with emotion. His hands dropped from her sides. ''Is something wrong?'' she asked.

He ran a hand through his silver-laced hair and began pacing over the old Turkish rug. He emitted a deep sigh. ''There's something else I'd like to say.''

A sense of foreboding ricocheted through her as she stared at him, in silence.

''One reason that I reacted so strongly to Lily at first was that she unearthed painful memories of the family I lost. There she was, all full of life and mischief and impossible to ignore. But you know Lily. She somehow manages to work her way into the most guarded heart.''

Erin couldn't help but smile, even though she ached with sympathy.

''But it's all right now,'' he said with a tinge of sadness. ''It was time I confronted things instead of burying myself in my work. When my old friend and mentor asked me to fill in for him while he was in Boston for a semester, I resisted. Then I realized that I simply owed him too much to say no.

''When I arrived, I'd made up my mind I was going to get away from things, watch the leaves turn and enjoy the peace and quiet, except that there wasn't any.''

Erin quirked a corner of her mouth. ''Sorry.''

He shrugged a shoulder. ''I understand. Nor was I your neighbor of choice. I've thrown your life out of kilter as well. But despite it all, I don't regret being here—at least not now. I'll be able to go back to Boston a better man for the experience.''

The mention of his leaving filled her with dread.

He took her hands in his. The soft lamplight played over the handsome lines of his face. ''You've been good for me, Erin. I've felt safe with a woman who didn't hold me in very high esteem, as odd as that may sound. And to be honest, the animosity was mutual. You were more spit and sass than I wanted to handle. But I'm happy we're friends now. I'm happy we like each other. Liking can be much better than loving. We both know how much losing someone you love can hurt. Love entails too much of a risk. It's not a risk I want to take again.''

A deep chill overtook her, cutting straight into her bones. She'd known the reality of their relationship all along, but his words made it even clearer. Perhaps he could go away with his heart unscathed, but it was too late for her.

She put on her bravest smile. ‘‘Don’t say that. The perfect woman may turn up someday, one worth the risk.’’

He grinned crookedly. ‘‘That’s what I like about you, Erin. You’ve got the right spirit about you.’’

She struggled to strangle a cry in her throat as he kissed her lightly on the cheekbone, his lips lingering for the barest of moments.

‘‘Good night and thanks for the cooking lesson.’’

Haltingly, she handed him Lily’s drawing as he walked out the door.

Erin turned her mind to business but in it she found little refuge. She had never expected anything from Wyatt but problems, and those she’d gotten, so why was she disappointed? His kisses had been filled with need, but it hadn’t been her that he needed. The yearning had been just that and no more. That he liked her and admired her way with Lily were of little consolation. She supposed he liked the queen of England and admired her as well.

To make matters worse, business had been very slow in the past two weeks. A large order for brass mortars and pestles from the Middle East had been canceled and a supplier for a rare type of stained glass had gone out of business. And in December, no one did much decorating. The business needed a shot of adrenaline and more exposure than just contacts could provide.

It was a story in the business section of the next morning’s newspaper that gave her the idea. She sat mesmerized, her eggs getting cold, as she read it. If a man in Iowa could sell vintage cars over the Internet, why couldn’t she put technology to work for her? She scrambled to the computer, quickly fleshing out ideas, some wild, some tame, all centered on a subscriber service, an import database for decorators around the country. It was going to take time, money, and travel, and maybe even a business loan, but this could be a breakthrough for her. Business, like love, was fraught with risks, but the rewards could be great.

She spent the day on the phone talking to a web-page designer, to her former employer, to decorating and import contacts. All offered encouragement. Mr. Karim suggested that she consult a lawyer as well. Her stomach tightened. It wouldn't—couldn't—be Wyatt.

December came gently under a cloudy sky and a breeze that bordered on balmy. But on the second day, the wind took a sharp turn to the north, bringing snow with it. It fell like confetti, a parade of white.

Erin wished for a yard of it. Snow kept people inside and that's where she wanted Wyatt to stay—inside his own house, away from herself and Lily. She wanted him to stay there until he left. She wanted him out of her heart, out of her mind, out of her sight.

But there was only about a half foot of it. The next morning, she waited until Wyatt had gone to work before she began clearing the walk—she with her large shovel and Lily with her toy one. But as they labored, she heard the sound of an approaching car. She looked up and found Wyatt entering his driveway. Her shoulders sagged. He wasn't supposed to be here.

He gave a brief wave, then entered the house. Erin waved back, her emotions raw at the sight of his dark, powerful form against the white drifts. Then she gave the shovel a cathartic plunge into the snow, scooping and dumping heavy piles until her arms ached and her lungs burned.

"Aunt Erin, leave some snow for me," Lily complained. She stopped for a moment to catch her breath, resting her mittened hands on the handle of her shovel.

Before she could regain her senses, Wyatt reappeared, carrying a thick, brown folder. Erin's heart wrenched as he turned toward them.

"Wyatt, I can shovel!" Lily announced. She scooped up a small quantity of snow and threw it up into the air.

A corner of his mouth tipped in amusement and he swooped her up with one arm. "What a busy girl you are. That must be why I haven't seen much of you lately."

His gaze shifted to Erin, again, sending her senses into a spin. His hair was ravenlike against a gray sky that hinted of more snow.

"We've been very busy," she finally managed to say, and told him briefly about her business plans.

"I've been busy, too," he said, with Lily's arm resting comfortably around his neck. "I ran off this morning forgetting a folder. We shouldn't let life be so hectic. We should slow down. They tell me that there's a man just outside the village who rents toboggans. How about taking the afternoon off and going for a ride?"

Erin tensed. "Thank you, but we really shouldn't."

"Aunt Erin, please," Lily said. "You promised we could ride a tobobbin sometime."

Erin took a pained breath and shot Wyatt a look of chagrin. Unfazed, he smiled at her.

Mr. Sorensen, a semiretired dairy farmer, had two-seaters, four-seaters and even a twelve-seater. They settled into a middle-sized one, with Lily in the front, Erin in the center, and Wyatt in the back as the steersman. Lily shrieked as the toboggan slid down the first hill, a modest incline deemed suitable for a four-year-old's first toboggan ride.

The exhilarating feeling of flight and freedom reminded Erin of her own childhood, but her heart was tethered to something more immediate. She couldn't escape the man sitting behind her, the touch of his body against hers, the conflicting emotions inside her.

They'd said little of any consequence on the way to the Sorensen farm. The exchanges had been mainly between Lily and Wyatt. They talked of preschool and what Billy Martin's arm looked like when the cast was removed. As Wyatt's rich laughter filled the car, Erin felt a mixture of pain and anger. A man who wanted no attachments shouldn't be spending time with a little girl who formed attachments easily. One broken heart in the family was enough.

Erin silently nibbled at the inside of her cheek as they swooped down one hill and climbed up the next with Wyatt pulling the toboggan. He gave Lily an assist with one hand while Erin held her other hand. With her red parka forming a dancing splash of color against the snowscape, the child appeared tireless, like a little clock that refused to run down.

As the toboggan slid to its next stop in a bracing rush of cold air, the light faded suddenly.

"Wyatt, there's not much daylight left," Erin said, climbing off. "I'm afraid we should be going."

"One more time," Lily begged.

Erin shook her head firmly.

The child's lower lip popped forward. "Please?"

Wyatt got out, clamped his hands around Lily's waist, lifted her out, hoisted her above his head, and spun her in a circle. She squealed. "Come on, Apple Cheeks," he said, lowering her to the ground, "your Aunt Erin is right. We can go tobogganing again some other time."

Erin flinched with anger. He had no right to say "we." There wasn't going to be another time with all of them. She watched with a leaden heart as he put Lily back in the sled and started toward the farmhouse. He reached out and draped an arm around Erin's shoulder, pulling her closer. The blood in her veins boiled, but her mind struggled in resistance. If Lily weren't behind them, she would have run—run into the snowy hills, out of his reach, out of his sight, away from his heated touch, away from his guarded heart.

They walked back in silence except for the small talk they made with Mr. Sorensen and a word or two about what an unusual autumn it had been. Erin settled Lily into the backseat. Once they were all inside, Wyatt turned toward her. Playful lights danced audaciously in his eyes. "So, wasn't this fun, after all?"

"Let's come back tomorrow!" Lily interjected before Erin could respond.

Erin said nothing. The merriment around her seemed to have a surreal quality—the laughter louder, the snow brighter—as if she were living a bizarre and unpleasant dream.

Wyatt started back toward the village. Erin was grateful, at least, that he made no promises, because when it came to tomorrow and all the ones after it, no promises could be made.

"Lily," he said, glancing at her in the rearview mirror, "let me tell you a story. It's about my great-grandfather who lived in Ireland a long time ago. He never rode a toboggan because it hardly snows in Ireland, but when he was a little boy, he would play the tin whistle day after day after day. He never wanted to do anything else. Other boys played outside, but he stayed indoors with his whistle.''

Erin turned to the backseat to find Lily leaning forward, her face tipped worshipfully toward Wyatt. Erin turned to him with a not-so-worshipful look, but he was annoyingly oblivious.

''And then,'' he continued in rich tones that seemed to be meant for storytelling, ''he became so good that he played in pubs in villages all around. My father made up a little poem about him for my sister and me. It went like this:

> He was an Irish lad
> When but a tad
> A tin whistle he could play
> Songs like birds'
> Songs without words
> All the live-long day.

Lily grinned widely. ''Tell me some more.''

''Well, one day, he stopped.''

''Why?'' Lily asked.

Wyatt looked at Erin with a wink. ''He discovered girls.''

Erin leveled a look of consternation at him.

He shrugged a shoulder. ''Well, what's wrong with that?''

''I have a grandpa,'' Lily drawled. ''He likes girls.''

Erin clamped the heel of her hand to her forehead.

Wyatt smiled as he looked at Erin. ''Oh, yes, the merry widower.''

''He sent us a postcard the other day from Key West,''

Erin said. "He's there with a new lady friend. There. I've saved you the trouble of asking."

"Thank you," he said lightly, pulling the car into the driveway.

He had barely brought the car to a halt when Erin thanked him and was out and unstrapping Lily from the backseat. Just as she pulled her free, she bumped into one of his long legs.

"Why are you in such a hurry?" he asked.

She groped for a truthful excuse. "Lily has school tomorrow."

He responded with a probing gaze that made her heart pound unnaturally.

She reached for Lily's hand, but not before the child could encircle one of Wyatt's knees and press her cheek into his leg. "Bye-bye, Wyatt."

Erin, with an ache spreading across her chest, dragged her away.

Lily was in such a state of excitement from an afternoon of tobogganing that Erin had to read her three bedtime stories to settle her down. Just as she was getting ready to turn out the light, the child abruptly sat up in bed.

"Aunt Erin?"

"Yes, Lily."

"Can Wyatt be mine and Wiggles's uncle?"

The entire room seemed to grow dark around her. "No," she said, her voice tight. "Don't even think about it. He has to go back to Boston. He has other things to do."

"But can't he stay?"

Erin felt a prickle of hurt as she looked into Lily's round, uncomprehending eyes. "No, Lily," she said firmly.

"We've talked about this before. Besides, we're not in the market for an uncle."

Lily rubbed her eyes ruefully, her small mouth pinched in a frown. Erin, the heat of anger and frustration rising in her, nudged her back against the pillow, tucked the quilt around her, and kissed her on the forehead. "Close your eyes and go to sleep. You'll feel better in the morning."

With a long, ragged sigh, Erin switched off the lamp on the night table and left the room, closing the door after her. Once out of the little girl's sight, she clenched her hands against her chest and mimicked a scream, a scream that she imagined reverberating off the surface of Mars. And if there had been anything to throw without waking Lily, she would have smashed it into a million pieces. Now Wyatt had really done it. He'd charmed Lily into heartbreak with his stories, rhymes, and toboggan rides. She'd warned him, but he'd ignored her.

She plopped into the rocker, rocking frantically and chewing the side of her index finger as she fought to hold back tears. How could Lily not notice that he was handsome and interesting and amusing when she hadn't been able to ignore it herself? She knew Lily was enchanted. But she hadn't dared to imagine that she had put him on the highest pedestal of all.

Erin was good and cranky after a sleepless night, and in a roaring mood to put Wyatt in his place. She'd show him just how good at that she could be. But she had to wait. The BMW disappeared from the driveway and the lights stayed off. On the second day of his absence, she called his office to learn he would have to make an unexpected trip to Boston. He was to return at the end of the week.

In the meantime, she had business responsibilities to attend to and she was grateful for the diversion they gave her. Leaving Lily with Tabitha, she drove to Brattleboro to meet with a web-page designer. A prototype that would later be the foundation of an on-line catalog would soon be completed. She made preliminary arrangements to make presentations to some of the major Boston design firms.

Lily seemed to understand that the idea of an ''uncle'' Wyatt was a forbidden subject, but she wanted to know why he wasn't at home. Erin gently reminded her that in less than two weeks, he would be going home to stay. And yes, she could give him a present, the misshapen but charming rendition of Wiggles that she'd made of clay. Erin suggested that they take it to a studio and have it fired.

On the day that Lily was at Mrs. Stahl's for an afternoon of sewing doll clothes, Wyatt came home. Stepping outside to get the mail, Erin caught sight of his car in the driveway and her breath hung in her chest. She dropped the mail back inside the mailbox and, without taking time to get her coat, she strode, heart pounding and arms swinging, to his front door.

The door opened before she could even point a finger at the bell. His sudden appearance not only startled her but left her suddenly speechless. Dressed in a black suit, white shirt, and a dark green print tie, he would have been a feast for any woman's eyes. The silver in his hair shimmered and his eyes reminded her of a summer sky at midnight.

The light in his eyes fading, he seemed to sense that hers was not a social call.

''You're not here to welcome me back, are you?''

She answered his question with one of her own. ''How could you just go away without saying anything?''

He arched an eyebrow. ''You noticed?''

''Hardly,'' she lied. ''But Lily did. You can't just show

a child the time of her life and not expect her to notice when you drop out of sight. She thinks you can spin the sun on the end of your finger.''

His expression darkened. ''I didn't mean to upset her.''

''Wyatt, you said you'd be careful. We shouldn't have gone tobogganing.''

His jaw hardened. He took her hand and pulled her inside, shutting the door closed behind her. He grasped her firmly by the shoulders and looked into her eyes. His face was within inches of hers. ''Just what do you expect me to do, ignore her?''

Erin's cheeks blazed. ''I expect you to back out of this relationship as painlessly as you can. Attachments are what children are all about. And you're a man who doesn't want any serious ties to anyone. You've said so yourself.''

His gaze burned into hers. ''She'll be all right. There will always be someone to take her tobogganing or to the fair. It doesn't matter if it's me or not. She's only four. She'll forget about me in no time. But if you think that once I cross that state line both of you will vanish from my memory, you're mistaken. I'm going to miss you—both of you.''

A lump rose in her throat. She didn't trust her voice to speak.

His hands dropped from her shoulders. He yanked his tie loose and unbuttoned his collar. ''There's not even time left for that button-sewing lesson you promised me,'' he said with a rueful smile. ''Let's not waste it fighting.''

''But there is time,'' she insisted. ''I said I'd show you and I will.''

''Erin, there's been a change in my schedule,'' he said bluntly. ''I'm going back to Boston in four days—to stay.''

Chapter Ten

Her heart slammed against her ribs. She studied his face as if it were a puzzle.

"My partners in Boston are down to the wire on an important case and need some help before it goes to court. Since my work here is all but finished, I volunteered." He explained it with irritating calm.

"That's what partners are for," she said, struggling to sound equally disaffected.

His lips tightened into a suggestion of a smile. "My exit should restore peace to the neighborhood."

She feigned a look of amusement, but inside, she was toppling under the weight of his words. His light treatment of the subject made her heart even heavier. "It's not the cause for celebration that you might think," she said.

His expression grew serious. "You're worried about Lily again, aren't you?"

She frowned. "Yes, and you should be, too."

He gave her a sharp look. "Erin, I meant what I said about keeping in touch. You and Lily and I—we can still occasionally do things together."

She swallowed hard. "I'm not sure that's a good idea, Wyatt. We should bring this to a close."

His jaw hardened. "Don't be stubborn. I can help you."

She tensed with anger. "I don't need any help."

A muscle twitched in his jaw. "Listen, if you're going to expand your business, you're going to need some legal counsel."

"I can get it here."

Frustration tightened his features. His gaze was intense. "All right, so you don't need me." He paused briefly. "But the offer still stands."

Erin, fearful that her facade of indifference would crumble at any moment, thanked him tersely, then ran home before the lump in her throat became too big to swallow.

The next few days passed with both painful slowness and alarming speed, leaving Erin feeling confused, conflicted, and battered by the emotional war raging within her. Sometimes she wanted him gone—banished to the dark side of the moon. Sometimes she wanted him here so she could feel the warmth and strength of his arms.

At this moment, she wanted him put on a ship bound for deep space. He hadn't said as much as "hello" to Lily since returning from Boston. He seemed to be avoiding coming into contact with either of them. He left early in the morning, not to return until after Lily's bedtime. Lily was disappointed and puzzled.

Not wanting it to be a sudden shock, she'd broken the news to Lily right away that Wyatt would be leaving early. There had been a hint of tears and a host of questions to which the answers were awkward and ambiguous, at best. But the child's eyes remained questioning. Erin was grateful that Mrs. Stahl, who had whipped up a pink "princess dress" for Lily's Barbie doll out of an old pair of curtains, had invited her back to make a crown.

She spent the afternoon working on details of a business trip to Boston and the presentation that she would give to prospective clients. She worked hard and long to take her mind off the man next door.

Erin awoke on a cold, blustery, overcast morning to find a moving truck parked in front of Wyatt's house. A cold emptiness filled her despite the efficient hum of the new furnace. Motionless, she stood behind the lace curtain like a gowned statue.

"Aunt Erin," Lily called plaintively.

She turned with a start as if awakened from an unpleasant dream. Behind her stood Lily in a long, pink flannel nightgown, and Wiggles.

"Good morning, Pumpkin," she said, reaching down and folding her into her arms. Outside, there was a metallic groan and a bang.

Lily slipped from her arms and went to the window. Erin's heart stumbled.

"He's leaving, Aunt Erin," she said with a hint of tears in her voice. "Wyatt's going away."

"I know, sweetheart," she said, smoothing her tousled hair.

"But I don't want him to."

"I know," she said, looking through the parted curtain, "but he has to."

Lily turned from the window. "I want to tell him goodbye."

"After breakfast," Erin said.

"Could we have some magic toast?"

"Yes," she said sadly, "we can have some magic toast."

Erin cut the toast in the shape of a star and covered it with grape jelly. She helped Lily into a red thermal knit

T-shirt and denim overalls. To cheer her up, she painted a small red heart on one cheek.

Lily returned to the window to watch, as she had that sunny August afternoon when Wyatt Keegan had made an unexpected and jolting return to their lives. How much had changed between them, Erin thought dismally, yet how much they remained the same.

Her heart pounded with dread as she got Lily's parka and mittens off the hall rack, along with Wiggles's mock Superman cape.

''Aunt Erin,'' Lily called from the dining room, ''here comes Wyatt!''

Her stomach knotted. She looked over her shoulder and saw Lily running toward the door, her face flushed. ''Can I answer it? Please, can I?''

''Yes.'' Her voice was tight.

On tiptoe, Lily flung open the door as Wyatt ascended the front steps. Dread swept through her as she watched him pluck Lily off the porch and hoist her into his arms. Then his eyes caught Erin's in a quick, blazing moment.

He set Lily down gently. ''I've come to say good-bye.'' He was without a coat, and wearing the denim shirt with the missing button. His black hair was tousled. It was with bitterness that she was again struck by how handsome he was.

Erin swallowed hard. ''Lily wanted to say good-bye to you. We were just on our way over.''

Wyatt, his hands on Lily's shoulders, looked down and smiled his crooked smile at the little girl.

Lily turned toward him. ''Do you really have to go?''

''Yes, Lily, I do. I have work to do at the courthouse.''

''You'll come back, won't you?''

His lips tightened. ''Yes, sometime I'll come back.'' He

seemed to be purposely avoiding Erin's emotion-laden gaze.

"What day is sometime?"

Wyatt's brow furrowed in discomfort. "I'm not sure, Lily."

Lily's eyes darkened. "But we have to go tobobbining again."

"Yes, we do," he said softly.

The child's eyes brimmed with tears. Erin's heart constricted. "Lily," she said, touching the child's shoulder, "let Wiggles out the back door and stay with him a few minutes. Then you can show Wyatt the dress that Mrs. Stahl made your doll."

She quickly bundled the child up and snapped on Wiggles's coat. Lily trudged toward the kitchen.

Wyatt looked at Erin cautiously. "Well, how did I do?"

She straightened her shoulders as if to give herself added strength. "She's trying her best not to cry."

He took her by the arms. His onyxlike gaze glistened with intensity. "Look, I'm not asking for the Nobel peace prize. I'm doing the best I can. I'm telling her the truth. I don't know when I'm coming back. But I will because I promised her. Face it, Erin. Aren't you being vague as well?"

Her cheeks warmed. "I don't know what you're talking about."

"Have you really explained to Lily that you don't want me in her life or yours?"

The tingle in her cheeks turned to flame. "She's just a child," she said defensively. "I'm trying to protect her. She gives with her whole heart. You have no heart to give back."

His expression turned to stone. His arms dropped to his sides. A cold silence fell over the room.

Erin suddenly realized that Lily had been outdoors longer than usual. "Excuse me while I check on her," she said, her voice tight.

She hurried through the kitchen and found Lily sitting on the back steps sobbing into her mittens. Wiggles sat next to her, his brown eyes looking sad and bewildered. Tears of her own sprang to her eyes.

"Oh, Lily," she said, sitting down and enveloping her in her arms. Wiggles jumped up and licked the child's face.

"I don't want him to go," she sniffed.

"I know." A lump that seemed to be the size of an orange lodged in her throat. "He's still here. Do you want to come back in the house and tell him good-bye?"

Lily pulled away and nodded, wiping her eyes on the back of her soggy mittens. Erin took a tissue from the pocket of her corduroy jumper and touched it to her cheeks. "We'll miss him at first, but things will get better. You'll see."

She took Lily's hand and helped her up. As they stepped back into the kitchen, Wyatt strode hurriedly toward them. "Is everything all right?" As he got closer to them, he stopped suddenly. "Lily, you've been crying."

Erin gave him a see-what-you've-done look. "Everything is going to be all right," she said for Lily's benefit, yanking off her damp mittens.

Wyatt crouched down on one knee and looked at Lily sadly, his head cocked and his chin crinkled. He held out his arms and she rushed into them. Erin's heart flew into her throat.

"Do you really have to go?" Lily asked.

Wyatt nodded. "No getting around it."

Lily turned to Erin. "But what about Wyatt's present?"

He gave Erin an awkward glance.

"Lily modeled a sculpture of Wiggles that she wants to give you," she explained, "but it hasn't been fired yet."

"I would be honored to have it," he said throatily.

Lily smiled for the first time all day.

"I can drop it by when I come to Boston," Erin said.

Wyatt's gaze snapped to hers. "You didn't tell me you were coming to Boston."

"It's a business trip," she said awkwardly. "Things just came together in the last few days."

He stood up. "When are you coming?"

"In two weeks."

"I want to see you," he said. "We have some unfinished business of our own."

"I've already told you how I feel."

His lips tightened. "If you don't call," he said obliquely, his hands on Lily's shoulders, "I'll assume you want to bring our friendship to an end."

Erin nodded, then turned away before she lost herself in the depths of his dark gaze.

"Well, Lily," Wyatt said, his voice injected with an unsteady cheer, "it's time that I go."

For an instant, it appeared that she was going to turn on the waterworks again, but instead, she bravely tucked her lower lip in. He picked her up and kissed her on the cheek.

"'Bye, baby," he said.

Lily hooked an arm around his neck. "'Bye, baby."

The lump that seemed to have taken up permanent residence in Erin's throat pushed upward again.

Wyatt put Lily down and took a step toward Erin. For a moment, she thought he was going to kiss her, but he stopped just inches away. His expression was solemn. The morning light streaming through the kitchen window had turned the silver in his hair to dancing lights. ''Good-bye, Erin. I'll await your decision.''

She responded with silence. He gave Lily a quick hug, Wiggles a pat, then strode away without looking back.

The image of his disappearing silhouette haunted her for days. She saw it as she worked. She saw it as she lay in bed at night trying to sleep. Her heart and her mind seemed to operate independently of each other. She yearned for him. Yet reason told her that to love a man who didn't want to risk love again was, after all, unreasonable.

Lily turned quiet and even Wiggles seemed to lose part of his spring. Erin, who struggled to maintain a facade of cheerfulness, sought to help her get her mind off Wyatt by sending her back to Mrs. Stahl's for another afternoon of sewing. She also took her to spend a morning at the general store helping Caleb care for baby chickens. But alone with her work, Erin found it even more difficult to forget. She couldn't forget his crooked smile, the way his hair fell over his forehead, and the feel of his rough jaw under her fingertips. She couldn't forget his wit, his spontaneity, and the way he held her in his arms. But she had to forget because she and Lily could never have a permanent place in his heart. That place had been taken by someone else.

All was in order for the trip to Boston. Lily and Wiggles would stay with Tabitha and Caleb for the three days that she would be gone. The sculpture of Wiggles, colored black and tan and having two large, slightly misaligned black eyes, was glazed and fired. Erin packed it carefully in a small box filled with shredded paper. If she chose not to see Wyatt, she could leave it with someone in his office.

* * *

She left on a cold, clear morning, on a commuter train that passed through a landscape dotted with barns and houses with smoking chimneys. An occasional wooden church steeple rose from among clusters of barren branches. Erin sat with her briefcase open on her lap, mentally rehearsing her presentation.

The train arrived just before ten, placing her in a city that was so familiar, yet so suddenly strange. She knew well the train station and the places where she had spent her years before Lily, but the buildings now seemed bigger, the noises louder, and the crowds denser than she remembered. She instinctively quickened her pace.

Within a half hour and a short taxi ride, she was at her hotel, a modest one set away from tourist attractions. She checked in and had a light lunch at a sandwich shop down the block.

Despite the presentations looming before her, thoughts of Wyatt played disturbingly across her consciousness. She could feel the nearness of him. In Maple Springs, she could feel his presence within her. In Boston, it was all around her as well.

The first of the presentations was that afternoon with an old client. Erin dressed in business attire for the first time in more than a year. She wore a red suit with a black collar and cuffs and black buttons down its off-center closure. With it, she wore plain, black pumps and simple silver earrings.

The presentations went well and so did the two the following day. The idea of an online finder's service and catalogue of hard-to-find furniture and decorating objects from around the world won unanimous approval. Yes, they all said, they would subscribe.

Erin took pleasure in seeing former clients and associates. They were full of questions about Lily and life in Vermont. She was delighted to win their support, but overshadowing her success was the knowledge that the time was drawing near when she had to make a decision.

Back at the hotel, she paced nervously on the carpet in her stocking feet. She called Tabitha and Lily to tell them that all was well and that she was on her way home. She assured Lily that she would deliver the ceramic Wiggles before she left.

Erin knew the answer to her dilemma. She knew that it was really no dilemma at all. Wyatt was a man who wanted to keep free of the heartache that love could sometimes bring. He was a man who refused to love again. Perhaps he couldn't love again. Perhaps his ability to love had died after his wife and child had died. So in that was the answer. There could be no happiness with a man with a shield in front of his heart. Erin wanted him to love her back and he couldn't. He could give her and Lily a little of his time and a little affection, but he couldn't give them his heart.

But that didn't keep her from yearning for him. Just that morning, her desire to feel his arms around her and to hear his voice once again was so strong that she'd placed a hand on the telephone and begun to punch in his number. Then she'd clapped the receiver down before finishing, her hand trembling, feeling like a foolish love-struck teenager.

She waited until the next morning—the last opportunity possible—to deliver Lily's gift. She boarded a bus and took it to an older and more fashionable section of Boston, with elegant brick buildings with deep, twelve-paned windows, wooden shutters, and doors with fanlights and gleaming brass knockers. Wyatt's office was in a three-story building with dormer windows. The window boxes were filled with cold-defying English ivy. A brass plaque next to the door read, "McGuire, Flaherty, Keegan and Winslow, Attorneys at Law."

Erin stood facing the building, her heart pounding in her ears, and steeled herself by breathing deeply. She went up the short flight of steps and rang the bell. A woman's voice came over the intercom. Erin identified herself, explained why she was there, and the door clicked open. She stepped inside to find an attractive gray-haired woman standing on the marble tiles in the entry.

She smiled at Erin. "I'm Mrs. Barnaby, the office manager. I'll ask Mr. Keegan if he can see you." She turned to leave.

Erin's stomach jerked into a knot. "No, please, that won't be necessary. Just give him this."

The woman looked slightly puzzled as Erin quickly handed over the small white box tied with red ribbon. She thanked her and hurried away.

As the train clacked toward Maple Springs, Erin's heart felt as though it would burst. She'd symbolically cut him out of her life. Why prolong the agony? It was the right thing to do, the only thing. Yet it felt so wrong.

Erin tried not to let it show, but an elderly woman sitting across from her gave her a sympathetic look. Erin managed a smile but it felt stiff and masklike.

As the train passed into Vermont, snow began to fall in large, lazy flakes. By the time it reached Maple Springs, the ground was covered with fresh ripples of white.

Lily and Tabitha were waiting for her at the station. For an instant, she forgot the pain in her heart, as Lily rushed into her arms.

The little girl put a wet kiss on her cheek as Tabitha looked on, smiling.

"I missed you," Erin said.

"Missed you," Lily said. She pulled away. "Did you give Wyatt my present?"

Her stomach tightened. "Yes."

Lily's eyes brightened. "Did he like it?"

She swallowed hard. "I left it with a lady in his office. I didn't see him."

Her face crinkled with disappointment.

"He'll love it, Pumpkin. I know he will," she said, her voice tight.

As she rose to her feet, Tabitha gave her a knowing look followed by a hug. "I'm so glad your business trip was successful, honey."

"Thanks, Tabitha."

The older woman smiled with pride. "Well, what do you say we scurry home? A big one's supposed to blow in tonight. Eight or ten inches on top of this, they're saying. Caleb's bringing in the cows."

They climbed into Tabitha's old Wagoneer and started on the short trip home. The snow flying against the windshield was in marked contrast to the calm gray sky in Boston.

"Aunt Erin, I milked a cow," Lily announced.

Erin turned to the backseat and smiled, grateful she wasn't asking any more questions about Wyatt.

"Caleb took her out early one morning and showed her how to do it the old-fashioned way," Tabitha said with a chuckle. "She was surprised it didn't come out cold like it does from the refrigerator."

"Wiggles and Tabby got into a fight," Lily said, continuing the saga of her stay on the Penobscot farm.

"Did either one of them get hurt?" Erin asked, mildly alarmed.

"No, but Wiggles started it," Lily explained. "He ate some of Tabby's food."

Tabitha glanced at Erin. "They was a-hissin' and a-growlin'. You'd think the world was coming to an end. Good thing I was there to stop it before it really got started."

Erin apologized. "Tabitha, I don't know how to thank you and Caleb for everything."

"Don't even mention it," she said, turning the wipers up to a higher speed. "We enjoy Lily. She brightens up the place. You know what I mean?"

Erin smiled. "Yes, I know."

They stopped by the Penobscot General Store to pick up Wiggles. Erin bought several bags of groceries in anticipation of the heavy snowfall and Tabitha drove them home. As she approached their bungalow, Erin's breath stalled at the sight of the saltbox next door, stark and empty in the winter storm.

Once inside her own house, she turned up the thermostat and put hot chocolate on the stove. The snow fell like a lace curtain past the windows, but instead of stopping to admire it like she usually did, she scarcely gave it any notice.

"Aunt Erin," Lily asked, standing in the kitchen doorway, "do you think Wyatt will come back soon?"

Her stomach tightened. "I don't know, Lily," she said chokingly.

"But he has to. He said he would."

"Yes, I know," she said, trying not to sound dispirited. Yes, he'd promised Lily he'd come back. But it was a promise that would be difficult for him to keep. And just yesterday in Boston, she thought with a painful twinge under her heart, she'd made it even more difficult.

Tired from the train ride and the pummeling she'd taken from her own emotions, Erin went to bed early. But she couldn't sleep. She turned on the light and began to read but she couldn't concentrate. Thoughts of Wyatt filled her heart and mind so fully that she was scarcely conscious of the howling of the wind outside her window.

She was startled when the telephone rang. She scrambled to her office to answer it, almost stumbling on the hem of her gown.

"Erin, this is Mrs. Barnaby from Wyatt Keegan's office."

She felt a dull pang of surprise. "Yes?"

"Dear, could you let me speak to Wyatt, please?"

Her hand tightened around the receiver. "I'm afraid there's been some mistake. He's not here."

There was a moment of silence. "But he left hours ago. He should have been there by now."

Erin turned numb. "When? When did he leave?

"Around five o'clock, just as soon as he could get away. It was beginning to snow a little, but he seemed determined to see you."

A fist tightened around her heart. "Mrs. Barnaby," she finally managed to say, "we're having a major snowstorm here, the kind you don't have in Boston that often."

"Oh, dear," she said after a brief pause. "Let me ring him on his car phone. I'm sure he's all right. There has to be a logical explanation for this. I'll call you back as soon as I can."

Erin stood frozen with the receiver in her hand. As a Vermont native, she well understood the dangers of driving in blowing snow, especially at night. Even the heartiest woodsmen avoided it. Finally, she set the receiver down, her heart banging in her throat.

The next few moments were an eternity. Shivering, she didn't want to leave the phone long enough to get her robe. When it did ring, the sound seemed to go right through her heart, like a spear.

There was alarm in Mrs. Barnaby's voice. "There's no answer on his car phone."

Erin's blood turned to ice. She tried to speak but couldn't.

"I'll alert the state police," Mrs. Barnaby said with managerial efficiency. "I'll also get back with the client who was trying to reach him. Try not to worry, Erin. He's very good at taking care of himself."

But she was worried. She was sick with worry. She slumped into her chair and placed her hands over her face. A gust of icy wind rattled the window.

She remembered being with her father and brother in a blizzard and how the snow bombarded the windshield in hypnotic swirls, making it almost impossible to see. But then, it had been in the daytime, and her father, seeing a familiar marker, the red smear of Mr. Hadley's barn, had turned off the road where they waited, bundled in blankets, until the storm subsided.

The route to Maple Springs was one of soft, lazy curves in the autumn sun, but in a winter storm it was treacherous. At night, it was deadly.

Erin bit her lower lip to hold back the tears. If something happened to Wyatt, it would be her fault. If she had agreed to see him, just been civil enough to talk to him just for a few moments, he wouldn't have come after her.

She went to the window, unable to see anything but snow swirling thick and threatening under a streetlight. Time seemed to stand still like a record stuck on one, long, dissonant note. The hands on the clock on her desk inched toward ten. Each minute was an eternity unto itself.

Trembling with cold and anxiety, Erin picked up the phone to call the state police herself when she saw a flash of headlights outside. Her heart lurching in her throat, she ran to the window to find a car inching to a stop at the curb. Under the shower of light from the street lamp, she could see a man's tall, broad-shouldered form against the snow. It was Wyatt.

With her pulse dancing and an unspoken cry in her throat, she rushed into the living room, threw open the front door, and, barefoot, bounded toward him through the snow. He opened his arms to her, lifting her off her feet.

"Oh, Wyatt," she cried, "I was so worried."

His lips touched hers, warming her all over. "This is certainly a better welcome than I got the first time I arrived."

"I would have died if something had happened to you," she said, kissing the tip of his cold nose.

"You're going to die if you continue to run around half naked and barefoot in the snow," he said, carrying her up the steps. "Come on, let's get you inside."

He set her down on a rug in the entryway and looked at her with a mixture of interest and disapproval. Her feet were red, the hem of her gown covered with snow.

Erin, her teeth chattering, self-consciously folded her arms across her chest. She'd been so crazy with worry, she had forgotten that she was wearing only a gown, even though it was a respectable one of red plaid flannel.

He smiled at her crookedly. "You'd better get some warm clothes on. Then you can ask me how my trip was."

By the time Erin had slipped into jeans and a heavy, red ski sweater, Wyatt was in the kitchen boiling water. He'd shed his heavy, black overcoat and wore a charcoal gray suit. His white shirt was unbuttoned at the throat and his dark red tie yanked loose.

She stood there a moment, drinking in the sight of him. "You're cooking," she said.

"No, you're cooking. I'm boiling water and haven't the faintest idea what to do with it except that I'm in the mood for a hot drink."

Erin smiled, taking his place at the stove. "I'll make some tea."

"You do that," he said, slipping his arms around her waist. "That's the least you can do. You put me through a lot of trouble tonight."

She turned toward him. "Oh, Wyatt, I never thought . . ."

Before she could finish, he took her into his arms and kissed her, first lightly, then with depth and conviction. She could feel his heart beating through his shirt while her own tripped wildly in her ears. When he released her, his dark eyes were murky with emotion.

"Mrs. Barnaby and I were afraid you'd been swallowed up by a monster snowdrift," she said, her voice thick.

The corners of his mouth tipped slightly. "I was concerned at some points that that would be my fate. This beautiful place has some awfully ugly weather. Once I realized that I'd gotten myself into a tight spot I slowed down to a crawl and was lucky enough to ride a good distance toward Maple Springs behind a snowplow. The only trouble was that it only went about ten miles an hour."

"Mrs. Barnaby said she tried to reach you by cell phone."

He grinned sheepishly. "It seems like I forgot to charge the batteries."

Erin sighed. "Call her right away. She's worried."

While he phoned, Erin brought two mugs of tea into the living room and turned up the thermostat.

Wyatt emerged from her office looking happy but tired. "All done." His tone was soft. "Lily sleeping?"

Erin nodded.

"How is she?"

"She misses you"

He swallowed hard. "I miss her, too. I miss both of you."

An ache coursed through her. "Wyatt, why did you come? You have to be crazy to take off for Vermont at night in a blinding snowstorm."

His gaze was intense. "A man has to be either crazy or in love."

Her heart kicked. "What do you mean?"

He pulled her into his arms. "I mean I love you, Erin. And I've also been crazy. After being away from you and Lily, I realized I was letting the past rule my life. Love is a risk, but I can't live without it anymore. I don't want to live without you and Lily. All the way here in the blinding snow, when I didn't know if I would make it, I realized how awful it would be to never see you again."

Erin's heart melted. "I love you, Wyatt. I love you."

He cupped her cheeks in his hands and kissed her forehead, her nose, and then the corners of her mouth until she ached in anticipation. Then he kissed her mouth with slow and lingering deliberation. He hesitantly pulled away.

"You know, I first thought that I loved you when you fell off the roof. You were so darned independent, yet vulnerable at the same time. You'd created a life for yourself and Lily that was so on-the-edge, unpredictable, and, well, interesting, and you'd taken sort of an odd pride in it. You aren't like some of those women who think they should be pampered and protected. I knew you could manage without me and I know you can now. But I want you, Erin,'' he said, stroking her cheeks with his thumbs. ''I want you to marry me.''

Her heart seemed to somersault inside her chest. ''I want to marry you more than anything.''

He kissed her again, then pulled her close and stroked her hair. Then he held her at arm's length, his eyes sparkling. ''Shall we wake Lily and tell her?''

Erin took him by the hand to Lily's room where she was sleeping with Wiggles at her side. Startled, the little dog sat up and emitted a yap. Lily's eyes fluttered open.

Wyatt sat on the edge of the bed.

The little girl sat up, rubbing her eyes.

''Hello, Lily,'' Wyatt said.

She looked at Erin, confused. ''Am I having a dream?''

''No, Pumpkin, Wyatt's really here.''

''And I'm going to be with you for a long, long time,'' he said. ''How would you like it if I became your uncle?''

Her eyes brightened. ''Yes, and would you be Wiggles's uncle, too?''

''Wiggles's uncle, too,'' he said, shifting his gaze to Erin.

Tears of happiness sprang from her eyes.

He took both of them into his arms and held them tightly and warmly as the snow blew against the windows.